Bedtime Stories for Kids

KINGDOM

Entertaining Stories to Make Your Children Sleep
Harmoniously

Jane Spark

TABLE OF CONTENTS:

GENEROSITY WINS

“They say, “If someone is meant to be together no matter whatever the circumstances are, they will be together in the end.”

Love is a very strong feeling, and when people fell, for some specific one, there is no going back, and they make sure to be the best one for that one person, to give their hundred percent in that relation to make it work and to stick together.

Similarly, In the town of Lakeville, there was a king and queen who had a very handsome son, named Bjorn. He was the pride and future of the kingdom as he was the only heir to the throne. Bjorn was popular in the kingdom as he was the most kind-hearted and down to earth Prince. He would spend his entire day in the kingdom and with its people. He was good at sports and loved doing horse riding as well. He, being a Prince, considered everyone equal and even sometimes used to spend his money on others as well. He always used to get scolded from his parents for being so generous to the town people.

King Rollo was considered to be harsh on people, to be in his limits with the people of the town and his son Bjorn turned out to be a different person and this was the reason the town people use to love him more than the king.

Prince Bjorn was also a very great fighter, and he was always ready for challenges and to risk his life to this extent that he did not even think about death. Bjorn was also into the work of trading, and he always used to travel to different places as a representative of the kingdom. It was more like trading was his passion.

He used to travel to the nearby tribes, but for the first time, he decided to go a little further from his kingdom. He planned to embark on a 2-3 days journey to the town of Yorkshire. He had heard the great news about that town and how people were getting new products from all around the world so he decided to visit.

He packed up all his belongings and other important stuff that he will be needing for the travel. He went for trading with some of his friends and started his journey. It took him an entire week to reach Yorkshire, and one night he finally reached there. Bjorn was even known there by a lot of people, and then, the town members informed the King and Queen of Yorkshire about him and he was asked to live with them at the palace.

Bjorn refused the request since he did not want any special treatment and did not want to bother anyone.

The king insisted Bjorn, "It would be an honor for us to serve a person with high character."

The king of Yorkshire was known to be very cruel to people, and not giving his people enough help when needed and also considered to be very selfish to others.

The reason to stop Prince Bjorn at his palace was to gain his trust and to trade with him rather than trading with other people in his kingdom.

A lavish dinner was organized for him where the king and queen joined him too. Bjorn told them his plan of staying for a while, and for what exactly he was in Yorkshire. The king and the queen asked him to stay with them for the rest of his stay and he agreed.

The next day, Bjorn went out for trading in the market and explored the market trends. He was observing everything with his sharp mind. He also sat with different people and noticed different factions and cultures. By the end of the day, Bjorn was able to make some friends that were ready to help him in trade.

It was late, as Bjorn spent a lot of time in the market. He went straight to his bed, to retire, without meeting the king. While relaxing at the terrace, he noticed a few people in the garden. He saw several girls in the garden too. He was a bit shocked because he didn't see anyone until now at the palace at this time. He saw girls passing by the garden very quietly so no one can notice them. Out of several girls, his eyes were hooked to a girl with blue eyes. It seemed as if the prince was lost in the beauty of the girl.

Soon the girls realized that they were being watched by someone, and all of them dispersed quickly. Bjorn tried to stop them as he wanted to know more about that blue-eyed girl, but he couldn't.

The prince spent the entire night thinking about the girl and her eyes. Seemingly, the prince was in love with her. He was curious to know more about her and decided to look for that girl in the morning.

The next morning, Bjorn started looking for that blue-eyed girl, and he looked everywhere in the palace, but she was nowhere found. Bjorn asked from his newly made friends about the girl, but they were not aware of any blue-eyed girl. The prince was curious as well as frustrated. He decided to stay longer to find out the whereabouts of the girl.

One fine night, he was again on the terrace sipping on a cup of tea. He looked at the sky and wished to see the girl again. Luckily, his wish got accepted. While he placed his cup back on the table, he noticed some movement in the garden. Bjorn immediately focused, and it was her. Prince silently walked to the garden and followed the girl to her home. Prince was adorned by the character of the girl. She was the care-taker and helper of the poor living on the streets.

One day, when Bjorn was out for trading, he noticed the same blue-eyed girl stealing things from traders and running away. Bjorn got very anxious to see this and wanted to know why would she be doing this. He walked to her house and decided to talk to her.

Prince knocked on the door of the girl and waited. After a minute, the door unlocked and the blue-eyed girl came out, "Yes?"

The prince asked, "Why are you stealing things from traders?"

The girl got scared, but remained calm, "I didn't steal anything. Why are you blaming me?"

"I saw it myself. Tell me the truth, or else, I will put you behind bars. I'm a prince," said Bjorn.

The girl noticed the guards standing beside the prince. She got even more scared and said, "What are you doing in the kingdom?"

"I asked you a question first! Why were you stealing?" asked Bjorn.

The girl walked close to the prince and said, "Come inside, I'll tell you everything."

Prince walked inside the house and commanded his guards to remain at the door.

The girl asked the prince to sit on the couch. Bjorn placed his sword beside him and started looking at the designs of the ceiling. Without wasting any more time, the girl said, "I'm the princess of this kingdom. My father is very cruel. He doesn't look after the needy people on the streets. This is the reason that I stole things from corrupt traders to help these people to fulfill their needs."

Bjorn found it strange and asked, "Why don't you talk to your father about this?"

"He won't listen. Moreover, he doesn't like me. This is why I spend most of my time in this secret place," replied the princess.

Princess took a break and asked, "Who are you?"

Prince stood up from the couch and replied, "I'm a prince of Lakeville. I came here to extend our trade network. I was about to leave the kingdom, but I saw you in the garden. I was astonished by your beauty, so I decided to search for you. And now I'm here."

Prince was impressed by the thinking of the princess and her bravery. They both sat again on the couch and continued talking.

Gunhild explained that she tried talking to her parents and ask them to stop being selfish and cruel towards the poor and help the poor, for a very long time she had to face a lot of issues regarding this problem but then with the help of her friends and some town people she managed to get away from her parents and started to fully help the poor people. The king and queen do still ask her to come back to the great life she has but she refuses as she knows her parents will not be supportive towards the poor or towards the one who is in need. The people of the town loved her and made sure to give her whatever they can give.

Bjorn was touched by her noble deed and was truly in love with her. He donated half of his earning from this trip to the poor people who were in need. He forgot that she was stealing things for a good cause. Gunhild was surprised to see what Bjorn did for the poor people and thanked him many times. Bjorn told Gunhild about himself and why he is here and where is he from. Bjorn asked Gunhild to spend some more time with him as he wants to know more about her and Gunhild agreed to this.

Daily at 5:00 clock, they met at a bridge place and then princess Gunhild showed Bjorn the town of Yorkshire. Daily a new place to explore. Bjorn was very happy to be with her, even Gunhild gave her information about all the traders of the town and who works how who is the honest one and a lot more. She wanted to help Bjorn and in this way she did. Bjorn ended making up more money.

The time came when Bjorn had to leave for his home as he had spent more than a month here as he was only in Yorkshire for 2-3 days but Gunhild made him stay for more time. Both of them were sad to be apart and the feeling of not seeing each other made them feel sadder. Bjorn wanted to ask her to leave with him but he wanted the things to get settled in some other way.

In a very short period, both of them got very close to each other and getting apart was very difficult for them but they agreed to see each other very soon.

Bjorn went back to his kingdom and Gunhild agreed to wait for her. Bjorn was sorely missed by everyone at Townsville. The people, his workers and even his parents too. Bjorn came back with lots of earning and his father was proud of him. Coming back to Townsville Bjorn started to focus more on his personal growth and started a lot of business for himself and started to earn better than his father. He spent months on this all and after some time he decided to tell his parents the love he had for the Princess Gunhild and how serious he is and he wants to marry her. His parents wanted him to marry someone from the family but he was so firm on his decision that his parents had to agree.

He again did all the packing for his trip to Yorkshire so he can make Gunhild his wife. He was very happy as he was going to see her after some months too. Finally, Gunhild and Bjorn met and Prince confessed the love he had for the princess. Princess Gunhild was very happy to know about it as she had similar feelings for Prince Bjorn but was waiting for him to come so she can finally tell her.

Now the hard part for them was to make Princes Gunhild's parents agree for this marriage. They planned to ask Princess Gunhild to go back to the palace and start living with her parents for some days and make their relationship better with her parents and she agreed to do that. Days passed by and things got better between her parents. That was the right time for Prince Bjorn to ask Princess Gunhild's hand from her parents.

Prince Bjorn went to Princess Gunhild Palace with lots of money and gifts for everyone and some expensive things for her parents and ask them to let him marry their daughter. They were shocked first as they did not expect someone like Prince Bjorn will end up marrying her daughter who is such a popular person around the town and people tend to be like him and people want as their King.

The King and Queen without any thoughts and hesitation said Yes to Prince Bjorn Proposal as they knew that they will not be getting anyone better person than him for their daughter. Prince

Bjorn took Princess Gunhild with her to Townsville. The wedding was one of the biggest weddings of that time, the entire kingdom was invited, everyone was given gifts and the food was disturbed among everyone. The Prince and Princess lived happily.

THE CURSED WEDDING

"There was a king who ruled a kingdom with his son and wife. The king was very polite, humble and kind. The kingdom was very happy with the ruler.

His son was very handsome and charming. He was tall, fair and had brown eyes. The prince was very generous, helping, loving and caring. The people of the kingdom were very happy with the king and his son because of their generosity. The prince had a beautiful voice. He loved to sing. He usually went to the grassland, near his palace, and sang lovely songs.

One day, a thought crossed the prince's mind that all his age fellows and friends got married but he still has no idea about who to marry. The king got old and, sooner or later, the prince had to rule the kingdom. The prince was lost and sad. He started living alone. There was an emptiness in his soul. He stopped singing and lost his beautiful voice in his thoughts. He started to live a sad life.

On the other hand, a princess lived in a neighboring kingdom. She was tall, pretty, as white as snow, and very attractive. She had long blonde hair. The princess always had a dream of a beautiful prince in her life. The princess heard many things about the neighboring Kingdom. She heard that it was a wonderland and had many beauty spots. She wanted to visit that beautiful kingdom just like a fairyland. She asked her father about visiting the neighboring kingdom. After a lot of requests and consideration, the princess's father permitted her.

The princess went to the neighboring kingdom for some days. When she reached there and saw the kingdom, she got very happy. The kingdom was as beautiful as the places she used to dream about. She started visiting different places in the kingdom. Every day she visited a new place in the kingdom. The people of the kingdom told her about the grassland. It was the same grassland where the prince used to sing the lovely songs in his beautiful voice.

One day, the princess went to the grassland. It was a coincidence that the prince was also in the grassland that day. The prince went to grassland after many months. Grassland was blooming with the beautiful flowers which also had refreshing fragrances. The sky was covered with clouds like mountains covered with snow. The birds were chirping and hence it was heaven on earth like scene. Everything was just perfect and presenting beautiful scenery. Princess had never seen such a beautiful place before.

The prince turned and his eyes began to shine. A beautiful princess with long blonde hair was standing there. She was looking gorgeous in her embellishing white dress. He had never seen such a pretty girl before. His heart skipped a beat. It was just like that prince had got his life back. The prince started singing for the princess in his beautiful and lovely voice. Princess listened to the beautiful voice of the prince. Prince had fallen in love with the graceful princess. The prince sang some lovely songs for the princess. They spent that evening together and decided to meet each other daily in the grassland. The princess went daily to the grassland to listen to the songs of the prince. She adored the prince's voice.

The days passed and they both had fallen in love with each other. Finally, the day came when the princess had to go back to her kingdom. During her last day in the prince's kingdom, the princess was very sad and upset. She went to the grassland to meet the prince. It was a lovely night. The sky was covered with shining stars and the moon which enhanced its beauty. She told the prince that today is her last day at his kingdom. The princess told the prince about her never-ending love for him.

Princess said, "*When I met you, a dream came true. You are the sunshine of my life. You light up my days. I cannot imagine my life without listening to your songs in the evening. You make me complete. You are the love of my life. My love for you is unconditional and eternal. You will stay in my heart forever."*

The prince also admitted his love for the princess. He said, *" I have been searching for someone to shake my soul. Then you walked into my life. You light up my life like the stars in the sky. You give me hope to carry on. You brought me out of the darkness. You rejuvenated in my faith, hope, love, and light. You are the one who put the music in my soul. You are the beat of my heart. I never knew what love was all about until I met you. I used to think there'd never be a girl who'd ever care for me. The sky was gray until I met you. We are under the same starry sky now. See the sky, See the stars, the starlight is back in the night, the moon comes shining down. Every star in the sky shines more brightly when you are at my side. When I look at the stars, I see us. You are the stars and I am the dark sky behind you. I think we have always been together even when we are apart. I will be with you from dusk to dawn."*

They were together under the same starry sky. They both expressed their love for each other and decided to get married.

The next day the princess went back to her kingdom. The prince sent the proposal to her dad for the wedding. Princess did her utmost effort in convincing her father for the wedding. After days of convincing, the princess's father accepted the proposal. They both started preparations for their marriage, and the day came when the prince went to her kingdom for the wedding ceremony. The prince brought the princess in his elegant palace as his bride. They started living a happy life. They both went to grassland daily, and the prince sang songs for her.

The king was very satisfied and relieved to see his son living a happy life, until one day, something terrible happened. One dark day, the kingdom got jinxed with a witch's spell. A wicked witch learned about the princess and prince happy life and decided to curse the princess because the king once rejected the witch's daughter's proposal for the prince.

The witch cast a spell, *"Abracadabra, may the everything in the kingdom dim! Abracadabra, may everything in the kingdom dim! Abracadabra, may everything in the kingdom dim!"*

It affected everything in the kingdom. The prince lost his beautiful voice and forgot how to sing. Princess's hair turned as dull as coal. The grassland turned into barren land. The witch deprived the kingdom of everything it had including rain, crops, sunshine. It was just like a nightmare for them. Everything turned dim and dark, which was very haunting for them. This state of kingdom saddened the prince and princess.

Eventually, the king got sick. There was no hope of his survival. Prince and princess used to get nightmares. Both the prince and the princess were helpless. They didn't see anything but darkness ahead. Life seemed to be scattered and falling apart.

One day, the princess saw in her dream that she was with her father and mother in a palace an old lady with white hair was giving her a ring and saying, *"Girl take it, take it, girl. It is a powerful ring. It has some special powers. Take it, girl. It will help you one day. Take it and use this ring during a hard time in your life. It is a magical ring. Take it, girl. You will remember my words one day"*

She woke up with shock. She had the same dream for many days but she had no idea about that ring. This dream was very disturbing and alarming for her. She only wanted to help the prince and people of the kingdom. So she decided to go to her father's kingdom and ask her father about that ring.

She went back to her kingdom and told her father about the whole situation and witch's curse. She also told her father about that dream and asked him about the ring. Her father told her that during her childhood she went to a kingdom that is far away from here. There they met an old lady. The old lady was sick and about to die. That old lady gave the princess a ring and told the princess that this ring would bring her special powers and help her in her bad times. The princess's mother who was the queen refused to take that ring, but the old lady forced them and gave that ring to the princess and told them about the powers of the ring.

The old lady told that there would be a time in princess life when everything around the princess would get dark and will scatter and will fall apart. There would be no other option except using this ring. The king told her that she was too young at that time so he gave that magical ring to her mother, the Queen. The princess went to her mother and asked her about the ring. Her mother gave her the ring and told her that the magic of this ring will only work if she wears this ring and dance. She had a hope that everything would be fine and the same as before after getting this ring.

She went back to the prince's Kingdom to help him. The princess told the prince about the magical ring and solaced him by saying that everything would be fine. The princess went to the grassland with the prince and wore that ring in her hand. The princess asked the prince to try to sing the same song which he was singing the evening when she first time met him.

At first, the prince could not remember the song. However, after the extreme effort and focus, the prince started singing the song in a bad voice. There was a glimmer of hope in his voice. He kept on singing. After some time, there was a beautiful echoing of his voice in the grassland. When the princess heard the song, she started dancing. The flowers in the grassland started blooming. The hair of the princess started to turn into their original color, blonde. Everything was getting better. The prince's eyes began to shine with happiness. The radiant glow of his eyes lit up the sky once more. The princess and the prince got happy because the ring showed its magic and everything was getting better. The prince recovered his beautiful voice back too. Both the prince and the princess went to the king and told him that everything is better as before.

The prince sang a song in his beautiful voice for king and he recovered. The king was relieved now. Everything in the kingdom got alright. The wicked witch was so angry that she flew to the castle and tried to curse the kingdom again.

She said, *"Abracadabra, Sim-Sala-Bim, may the rose's color dim!"*

The princess's hair turned as dull as tar again. Only this time the witch also picked up all of the roses in the entire kingdom.

The witch once again said, *"Abracadabra, may everything in the kingdom dim! Abracadabra, may everything in the kingdom dim! Abracadabra, may everything in the kingdom dim!"*

She sneered, filled with rage.

"Let's see how you'll break my curse now!"

The princess used the same ring and asked the prince to sing the same song once again any everything got normal in the kingdom. The kingdom was restored to its original glory because of the princess's efforts.

Upon learning that her curse had been broken again, and she could never ruin the kingdom, the wicked witch's evilness swelled so much that she exploded into a thousand tiny pieces. Eventually, rose blooms sprang up in the grassland in the kingdom once again. Princess and prince began to go to the grassland every day again and the prince continued to sing songs for the princess as he used to and they started to live together happily after.

A METALLIC BOX

66 There wasn't a single cloud in the sky. The sun was huge and red, shining to its fullest. It was a normal July afternoon. Just like everyone else, the hot weather forced James and Mary to stay inside their house, safe from the heat.

Unlike most boys his age, James had longed for holidays from school all year long, not because he wanted to play in the park with his friends from the street or because he wanted to watch the TV all day long but because he wanted to relax and read books and do what his heart desired him to do. And now since it was summer vacations and he was finally free from any schoolwork, James decided to paint and decorate his room wall. His room was very well kept and organized. With all his favorite childhood storybooks and toys neatly placed in the big closet on one wall, and his bed and study table placed side by side on the other, James loved the tiny space he called his room. He had a big window on the wall where his study table was placed and loved to sit there and look at the plants and the trees in the park while studying. Spending most of his time in his room, his parents had noticed on various occasions that James was a quiet boy who liked to keep it to himself. So, they always suggested to him activities that he could easily do on his own, have a good time and learn something new as well all the while. Painting and decorating his room wall was one of their suggestions and James liked it better than the rest of them. He always wanted to make his room feel and look a little more colorful than it did now. And so, with the paints his granny got him as his 12th birthday gift, James set to work.

Mary, a chirpy three-year-old, has always been very fond of his big brother. She followed him everywhere. With big round eyes, she observed his every action and tried to mimic them to the best of her abilities. She had already adopted a lot of James habits as their mum always said.

James picked up a paintbrush and drew an arched line. This will be the head of the giant caterpillar he planned on making. Mary tried her best to do the same. She picked the biggest paintbrush, dipped it in the bottle of the black paint, then water, then paint again. With shaky hands, she stretched out a crooked line on the paper James had given him. Done with it, she showed it to him, expecting appreciation. James clapped in return, making her laugh. They both adored each other.

An ice-cream truck passed by in the street. They both instantly looked up and at each other, both breaking into a big smile. They rushed downstairs to go outside and stop the truck. Both asked for the ice cream they wanted. As soon as Mary got her ice-cream, she started to walk back inside. James waited for the change.

While walking inside, Mary looked to her right and found that the door in the garage ajar. It was left open by her parents. Feeling excited, she started walking inside. James walked in at just the right time to see this. He rushed behind her, worrying she might hurt herself because she is too young to roam around on her own.

It was a storeroom. Loads of cardboard boxes stacked on each other against each wall. They all had labels on them. Some read "kitchen", while others have "books", or "living room" or "bedroom" written on them.

One metallic box, lying in the corner, caught Mary's eye. She picked it up. It was lighter than she was expecting it to be. The box had a lock on it, which made Mary curious about what would possibly be inside. James walked in at the same time. He took the box from Mary and just as he was putting it back to its place, his inner voice told him to open it. The lock on it asked for a combination of four numbers.

James randomly put in 1, 2, 3 and 4 but the box didn't open. Curiosity filled him almost instantly at that. As he thought of more combinations to try, the unusual scratches on the corner of the box grabbed his attention. There were four of them. One shaped like a square, the other formed an arrow. The third scratch looked like a deformed circle and the last one, a triangle.

A square, an arrow, a circle, and a triangle. What could that possibly be?

James stared at them for a little longer, just to realize that these could be hints to the passcode of the box. The owner of the box might have written them in case he forgot the real combination.

As James was deep in his thoughts, he noticed that this one cardboard box on the top shelf had a big square drawn in red marker on it. He looked at the metal box in his hands, the two squares very identical.

"Maybe that box has a clue to the combination of this box." James thought to himself.

He used the stack of boxes on the ground to make a stair and climbed up to the top shelve. He reached out to the cardboard box and opened it. There were kitchen utensils inside. He then turned the box over expecting to find some number written on it but there was none. Anyways he brought the box down and placed it next to Mary who was busy eating her ice-cream.

Then he took a walk around the store, looking for boxes with the rest of the clues drawn on them. There were none, except for a glass piece shaped like a cone. A triangle.

He picked it up and handed it over to Mary, telling her to be careful with it and not to break it. Mary, done with her ice-cream by now, took the task given to her very seriously. She was looking at the crystal triangle in her hand with awe when its base clicked open. Something fell to the ground. It was key.

"I didn't do anything Jamie" Mary explained, filled with guilt that she broke the triangle.

James smiling at her picked up the key-shaped like an arrow.

"This is it! This is the key to the box." Overwhelmed with excitement, he quickly remembers that the box didn't have even have a keyhole. It opened with a passcode. With this thought, he put the key in his pocket and went on to look for the last hint, the circle.

After an effort of ten minutes and failing to find anything circular, he sat against one of the cartons when he suddenly noticed that the clock on the wall was not working but all the needles were perfectly aligned on each other and pointing towards one number only.

Two.

It hit him at that moment that the clock was a circle in shape!

"That's it! That's the last clue!"

So, a box with kitchen items, a glass cone, a key, and a clock. What numbers were they telling? As James went back in his thoughts, his sister pulled out the kitchen utensils.

Mary, who had just recently learned how to count till ten, started to pick each item and put them back in the box.

"One..." She went as she gently threw the spoon back into the box.

"...two..." There she put the knife.

"...three..." the peeler.

"...four..." another knife.

"...five..." the fork.

"...six and the last." She called while putting the lemon peeler back in.

"Six Jamie Six."

"These are six." Mary excited to have counted correctly, told it her brother.

Hmmm, six James wonder as he pats Mary on her head. Maybe that was one of the numbers of code. And in fact, it was. Finding another number motivated James to search for the remaining two. He was halfway there now.

He started observing the cone closely but failed to find any number or anything hinting towards a number, so he took the key out of his pocket.

The arrow key had a very clear number "Nine" carved on it.

"This one was easy." James thought.

He went back to observing the cone. Now it occurred to him that there was no number written on the box, but the number of items in the box was possibly hinting a number. What if the number of corners of the cone was a digit of the password? He started counting them. There were eight of them.

"Two, Six, Nine and Eight." He put these numbers on the lock, but it didn't open. Disheartened a little, he arranged them in the order of the shapes drawn.

Six from the carton with the square on it.

Nine from the arrow-shaped key.

Two as the needles of the circular clock pointed.

And finally, Eight from the corners of the triangular cone.

"Six, Nine, Two, Eight." The box clicked opened.

Inside the box, James found a book and a photograph.

He took out the book that looked like someone's old journal. As soon as his hand touched the old rusty book, he felt tiny grains of dust on his skin. The outsides of the journal looked tough, with edges of some pages peeking out from the corners of it. He tried to think of the age of it. It must be as old as the ones my granny kept in the drawer beside her bed and cried a little whenever she read them. Her mother had told him that those old books once belonged to grandpa and granny read them only when she missed him. He saw granny reading them quite a lot of times. "then granny must miss him quite a lot of times", he thought to himself. So, this must be my grandpa's too! A strange type of excitement filled him. He opened the journal carefully; afraid the cover and the pages might crumble to dust. He opened the first page. Some jumbled up alphabets were written there in a handwriting Jamie found hard to read. He tried to make sense of them but failed. He moved onto the next page, hoping that something is written there might speak to him and reveal the identity of the journal. But on the next page, Jamie found more jumbled up alphabets, one group following the other till the end of the page. He tried to read them but could only make out some words like "the house", "wife", "to", "my children", "a", "and"; word that he understood but failed to match with the rest of them. He turned another page, a similar thing happened. Some words he understood, most he didn't. The identity and the author of the journal still lost on him. He kept opening random pages, ran his fingers on the words he couldn't understand until he lost heart and set the book down, moving onto the next item.

He then picked up the photograph. It had a house with walls painted brown and a shiny red door. Trees were surrounding the house and a small pond with ducks in it. Whose house could it be? When he looked at it a little longer, he realized that it was his house, and they were so much the same and different.

The trees that made the view look fresh and pleasant were no longer there. Instead, now there just stood dry grass. The pond with ducks in it was replaced by a small cemented pool that Mary sometimes sat in. The building of the house was now a bright yellow, but the door was still the same. Seeing how the greenery had made everything so much more beautiful, James immediately decided to spend the rest of his summer vacations planting trees in the garden.

DRAGON SLAYER

"Once upon a time, in a far-flung land, where witches flew around on their brooms and ogres looted the land. There was a kingdom of the great Lord Zeus. After an endless battle, Lord Zeus was able to establish a city where peace diffused throughout the land. The citizens never saw the sight of blood or carried hate and lust in their hearts. On one magical day, the ogres and witches made a pact with Zeus, where they agreed that they will not disturb the peace of the kingdom if the army of Zeus stops hunting the ogres and witches that stumbled near the circumference of the realm.

From that day onward, everyone lived with happiness and joy except a very wicked witch which burned in the flames of revenge. She wanted to take vengeance from Zeus as he had killed his one and only daughter, Shiela. She kept on planning ways to hurt Zeus or his kingdom. She was ostracized by other members of the witch community when she tried to instigate them to break this treaty.

"Woe you Zeus, Woe you!", she kept yelling it day and night.

Soon, Zeus was married to Lady Theodora of the house Mendrili. Flowers blossomed and the city swelled with fragrance and visitors who wanted to see the Royal wedding. Of course, the witches and ogres came to this auspicious occasion to witness to kingdoms merge into one.

The guests would ask the magical mirror, "Mirror…Mirror on the wall, who is the prettiest of them all?" and the mirror would reply "Lady Theodora." Certainly, the mirror did not lie because Lady Theo had golden bright hair and deep blue eyes. The locals described her as, "Beautiful and ever-youthful." Zeus fell in love with her at first sight. The aisle of the church was filled with flowers, when the doors suddenly flung and Lady Theo in a gleaming wedding dressed entered the hall. Silence fell among the audience. Everyone stared at the beauty and grace of these women. The royal wedding proceeded and soon the newlywed couple was off to Arizona.

Meanwhile, the evil witch continued to plot.

After a couple of years later, a wave of joy swayed through the kingdom again when this news was announced:

"To the people of Winsdale, it is of great honor and pride to tell you all that there is a new addition in the royal family.

The king has been blessed with Prince Jacob. The king expects you all to pray for his son and celebrate this occasion."

The city went wild. Everyone rushed to the castle to see this baby boy. Shop vendors gave away free things and fireworks were arranged. It felt like a festival. People hurriedly gathered the lanterns and wrote blessings and prayers for the newly born prince on it. The night looked like a day. This celebration lasted for three days. Witches brought magical gifts while ogres brought expensive loots and presented this at the disposal of King Zeus.

However, the birth of the prince provided the wicked witch with the perfect way to take revenge from Zeus. She recently came up with a spell to shapeshift. She entered the city and went to the castle to pay respect to the king and queen as well as this newborn. She noticed that the prince was being handled by Edna, middle-aged chubby women. She went to Edna to begin to talk to her and then she cursed her with the spell of sleep. She was able to this without being noticed by anyone. She then dragged sleeping Edna and locked her into a room. Then she shapeshifted as Edna and came closer to Baby Jacob. She pretended that the baby needs to be changed and headed to the royal quarters along with a team of all the other caretakers. As soon as there was nobody around her, she chanted the spell making everyone fall to sleep. Then she escaped from the city and took baby Jacob to her lair. According to the legend, it was said that the son of the preacher of peace will be a source of strength and power. Since now the baby was with the wicked witch, she was the most powerful among all the witches.

The town drenched in sorrow. Every one searched for the lost one but nobody could find that out. The witches were called on to formulate a spell that can trace the lost prince. Of course, the witches promised to help but spells took eons or at least years to be drafted and used. Lady Theo lost her vision as she cried day and night for her lost son. King Zeus went on expeditions to find his heir but failed every time. Years passed and eventually, King gave up hope.

On the other hand, the evil witch begins to train Prince Jacob in archery, horse riding, fencing, and magic. She treated him like a son and would warn him that if he got out this lair, he would die or the people would kidnap him and put him on stake. He did listen to her but prince Jacob was very mischievous, he would often go out of the lair to see a Huge castle at a far off distance. He made friends with the goblins and dwarfs and became very famous in their communities. The witch would often tell Jacob stories of dragons, giants, and mermaids. This created a spark of desire in Jacob's heart to keep a dragon as a pet. But then as he grew up, the goblins told him that:

"Anyone who shall kill Dragon of the Targaryen will be the king of the world as well as the king of the ogres."

Jacob was well aware of the world but was still oblivious of his actual identity. He had met other witches, ogres, mermaids as well as the other fanciful creatures. He was well regarded for his valor and bravery. No one recognized him as the witch was able to transform his blonde hair into black. There was no way one could guess the royal blood flowing through his veins.

As days went by, Jacob started working hard with one aim mind; I need to defeat the dragon. The witch, who had developed motherly emotions for Jacob, supported him and asked a few of the centaurs to train him for this.

After a few days, Jacob only went to return as the "Dragon Slayer". The fight had been intense but what mattered was that now the head of the Dragon of Targaryen was in front of the ogres. All the ogres bowed down to accept Jacob as their king.

For a kingdom to prosper, the witch recommended him to marry a princess. Jacob realized that if he marries the princess of Gamseth, then he will gain more support in humans too. He was able to impress the Lord of Gamseth on an archery competition. He shot three consecutive arrows on the bullseye, whereas the other princes or kings were not able to hit even a one-shot. The Lord himself asked him to marry his daughter. The marriage turned out to be a great success. The ogres were able to develop an army and their loots were organized, all under the supervision of Jacob. He turned out to be a great administrator and a warrior. The ogres welcomed their Queen, Fiona.

Life went back to normal but then an army of ogres crossing through Zeus kingdom was killed. Jacob was impulsive and sent a letter asking to punish the killer or be prepared for an attack. King Zeus did not respond to this warning instead prepared for war. Jacob knew he had to perform well as it was his first battle after all. He turned his castle into an armory. Ogres knew the pact had been broken and now they can go back to wilderness. Witches remained neutral.

Jacobs troops laid a siege on Winsdale. The royal army hurled stones and boulders on the ogres resulting in causalities. But the ogres were far more in number and stronger than the royal army. They launched the catapult and cracked the boundary of Winsdale. The wicked witch chanted spells killing many soldiers. No man could stand his ground against Jacob. On the other hand, Zeus had hired an alchemist to build a bomb. He planted the bomb in places where Jacob could most likely attack. He planned to drive the ogres toward a very steep ditch through these bombs. To his surprise, these bombs were very effective in killing these huge, hideous creatures. His plan had worked out but he had also underestimated his son's skills.

Jacob had a backup troop which comprised of the best soldiers of Gamseth, highly trained centaurs, smart goblins, and the witch. While the bombs were killing the majority of the ogres, Jacob led his back-up army to the same castle he was born in. Only a few soldiers were present there for the protection of the Queen and Zeus.

Before going to the throne room, he saw something unusual. It was a symbol that resembled the tattoo he had on his ribcage. He ignored all this and ran to kill Zeus. The Queen was already moved to a secure place but Zeus sat bravely on the throne when Jacob entered.

"Looks like you are either waiting for me or death!" said Jacob.

"I await none", said Zeus in a thunder-like voice. His age sure was old but his bravery was still the same. He stood up, swung his sword and charged. Jacob already predicting the situation, Charged with the same energy. They kept fencing each other until Zeus left a huge scar at Jacob's abdomen, exposing his ribcage and the tattoo. Zeus saw the tattoo and misinterpreted the next attack. Jacob had his sword crossing through his father's heart in the next minute.

Zeus collapsed to the ground but before he gave up on the life he said: "Be good my son!"

Before Jacob could interpret what had happened, few men entered the courtyard and killed the witch by separating her head from the body along with a few goblins. With the witch dead, all her spell halted, exposing the blondeness of Jacob. Before Jacob could do anything, a man from the troops said, "Drop the weapons! He is the missing prince".

Everyone dropped their weapon and bowed to the new king Jacob. Everybody kept exchanging looks between the tattoo and Jacob. Jacob tried to question what was happening when more people entered the room and bowed down to Jacob. A very weak and ancient man came out from the crowd and announced:

"Welcome back home! Prince Jacob, son of the Great Zeus, The Peacekeeper."

Jacob just stared at the man's face and then looked to see the corpse of his mother. Then the priest continued to tell him that only the members of the royal family have this branch of olive near the ribcage. Plus, the members of this family contain blonde hair. Jacob was still skeptical when this man rushed to the dead body of Zeus. Jacob realized that the man he had just killed looked just like him. He let out a shriek of anguish. The kingdom of Zeus accepted Jacob as their new king.

The Queen was informed and brought to her son. She was blind but with one touch on Jacob's forehead, she was able to recognize that he is her son. She began to cry as she embraced her son. Jacob realized he lied his entire life and that he killed his father. But time heals the wound over time. Jacob brought his wife and contributed to improving the relationship between Winsdale and Gamseth.

Peace prevailed all over the land. Flowers that had turned to dust, begun to bloom again.

THE ROYAL ELEPHANT

"Faraway in the foreign land, lived a king in his huge castle. Everyone in the nearby village knew that the king was a kind, just man who not only showed mercy to his people but also the animals. Being very fond of animals, the king decided to pet an elephant. Out of love for the elephant, he made sure his craftsmen make a huge, comfortable stable for his elephant.

Years passed by, and the elephant became famous as the "Royal elephant" in the village. People used to stop by his stable now and then to pet him as the royal elephant as they thought of him being the lucky charm for the village. Everyone adored him. There was a stray dog in the village too. His name was Oreo. Nobody wanted to pet him and that is why he used to starve for many days and no one would even notice. He used to go to the dustbins in the search of food and used to eat whatever was leftover or useless to people. Nobody gave him attention and therefore he never got a proper bath or shower. Nobody cared for him and to make the situation worse for him people used to hit Oreo with stones to make him run away from the place because he was dirty and filthy as he never received proper care.

One could see his ribs on his body and see how weak he was. On one bright sunny morning, Oreo, accidentally, went to the royal elephant's stable. The Elephant got surprised and angry because he did not like dirty and filthy being around him, the royal elephant started jumping out of aggression. Noticing the hostile behavior of the elephant, Oreo barked at him and ran away. After a few days, Oreo stopped by the stable again. The royal elephant started to get annoyed and jumped out of frustration. But today, Oreo didn't bark at the elephant because he had seen something else the stable! There was a huge, black snake right behind the elephant!

Royal elephants' anger grew as he saw that the dog was not leaving his stable. He stomped his feet even harder to make the dog run away. Oreos's mind started racing as he was thinking of ways to save the elephant from the big black snake. Luckily, a bright idea struck his mind. He decided to run towards the snake, and an elephant saw that the dog is not leaving his stable, his anger grew further. As Oreo ran towards the scary snake, the elephant followed him and stomped even more aggressively. As a result of the royal elephant stomping, he stepped on the snake and killed it. Now the royal elephant realized that why Oreo had run into the stable, and not outside. Oreo had made the elephant follow him and step on the snake so it could die! Realizing that, the Royal elephant thanked Oreo and befriended him. Oreo saved the elephants' life!

From that very day, Oreo used to visit the royal elephant's stable more often and they became best friends. The royal elephant used to share his food with Oreo and they used to talk about their day over supper. The elephant got so friendly with Oreo that he even showered water over him with his long trunk. This way, the royal elephant didn't feel lonely in his stable and started to feel happier. Oreo had started to become healthier and better, even the villagers noticed that too. This was because the elephant used to share his food with Oreo and he did not have any need to go to dustbins in the street to find leftover unhealthy and unclean food. One of the villagers was keen to keep the dog as a pet. He was among the same people who used to throw stones at him and hated him. So, he went to the stableman to make an offer. He asked the stableman if he could sell the dog to him as he was healthy now. Stableman had no right to sell the dog to the villager as he didn't own the dog but he grew greedy and wanted to negotiate. The villager offered him a few gold coins in exchange for the dog and took away Oreo.

Days had passed away, and Oreo had not visited the royal elephant. The Royal elephant started to get sad and used to cry every day. Since he was used to having food with Oreo, he had stopped eating at all and became weak. The king got worried about his elephant too. He summoned the stableman to his castle. Stableman got very frightened that the king will get very mad at him if he told the king that the elephant's health is on stake because of him. The elephant was not feeling well because he could not see his best friend Oreo. The stableman thought of an idea to tackle the anger of the king. He thought that if he will not tell the king about selling the dog, who was elephants' best friend than the king will not blame him for the deteriorating health of his beloved elephant and will think that some disease might have made the elephant weaker. The stableman went to the royal palace and went straight to the throne where the king was sitting.

The king asked the stableman, *"O stableman! You had the job to take care of my beloved elephant but you are failing to do so. I see his health deteriorating every day. Don't you know how lucky the elephant is for this kingdom? What is the reason behind it?"*.

The mischievous stableman replied *"O My Lord! The greatest of all the lords! The caring and beloved King of this kingdom! I would request you to allow me to defend myself and explain to you the real matter."*

The king agreed and proceeded to say, *"Your Highness! I used to keep the lucky elephant very clean and I used to feed him now and then and I treated him very well. Then one day the elephant stopped eating food and he hesitates from showering. I do not know exactly why the elephant is not eating properly but what I think is because he does not shower therefore some disease has attacked the elephant which does not allow him to eat food."*

The stableman lied to the king that some disease had attacked the elephant. Although, he knew the real reason that the elephant is not feeling well because his best friend Oreo was missing and Oreo was missing because of him.

A royal vet was called by the king and he was paid large amounts of money to treat the royal elephant. The royal vet spent days and made numerous medical potions for the elephant to drink. Sadly, none of them worked and the royal elephant was still sick. The king was now stressing out as nothing made the royal elephant better. One day the king himself decided to visit the stable and take a look at the elephant himself. So, he visited that stable and saw that the elephant started crying as soon as the food was brought near him and he saw his food. The king himself got sad for once when he saw the elephant crying. The very next morning, the king held an advisory meeting and asked his advisors to advise him suggesting different ways to help the elephant. One of them told the king that he heard from the villagers that there is a dog that used to visit the stable often and used to spend a lot of time with the elephant but he had disappeared all of a sudden. This made the king wonder and he got curious and he called the stableman to his castle once again. The stableman got nervous this time because now he had a suspicion that maybe the king now knows about the dog he sold and the king might ask him about the dog this time.

The stableman arrived at the Royal Palace and the king asked him, *"O stableman! We have heard about a dog who often used to visit our lucky elephant and they were good friends. Is this true?"*

The stableman got embarrassed and replied, *"O my lord! I am extremely sorry for such careless behavior and yes this is true. Please forgive me!"*

The king got infuriated and asked, *"Where is that dog?"*

The stableman replied *"Oh your Highness! I sold it to a man in this village."*

Like this, the king got to know that he had sold the dog for merely a few coins! The king was furious. He fired the dishonest stableman and appointed a new, nobleman as the new stableman. After analyzing the whole situation, the king called the chief minister and asked him to come up with a proper solution as he could not see the elephant sick and sad anymore. The royal elephant had stopped eating at all and as a result, had gotten very sick. The chief minister came up with the solution that a prize should be announced in the village, anyone who would find the dog and handover him to the king would be awarded a sack of gold coins! The villagers took upon this opportunity with enthusiasm and started searching for Oreo. The man who had bought the dog heard about the prize immediately ran to the castle. He met with the king and told him that he had bought Oreo with pure intentions and loved the dog. The king assured him that Oreo will be taken care of and would be loved. Moreover, the king assured him that the money he paid for the dog will be returned too. The man got happy and promised to bring back the dog.

The very next day, Oreo was brought back to the stable! The king himself welcomed the dog and petted him. The king took Oreo to the stable. Once the elephant saw his best friend Oreo, he got very excited and happy! The elephant jumped and blew his trumpet in happiness. Oreo also ran around the elephant with joy and happiness. King got very happy to see his lucky elephant happy and smiling and he was relieved to think that the elephant will not cry now. The king that day understood the real importance of true friendship and he got tears in his eyes of joy. The royal elephant had now started eating food regularly and was not sick anymore. Oreo and the elephant lived together, played together and ate together. The whole village was a witness to their friendship and was in awe.

Several years passed by and the older generations still narrate the symbolic friendship between the elephant and the dog. Both of them could not even live a single minute without each other. The story teaches us several lessons. For example, the importance of friendship, sincerity, and love. Moreover, we are taught how dishonesty is wrong and honesty must prevail to maintain peace in society. We saw how the stableman was not honest and he lost his job. Moreover, the man who had bought Oreo was nice and honest and returned him to the king. This way he not only got respect and appreciation, but he also golds coins as a reward!

THE TWO PRINCES

"In a land far away, there was a king whose wife had died in childbirth, leaving behind an infant son, the Prince Harry. When the prince was nearly grown the king married again, this time to a woman who also had a son, and his name was john. The stepmother became the new queen, and her son became the Prince john.

The new queen felt enraged and envious because the king's son harry was far more handsome, taller and stronger than her own son Prince john. She could not bear the thought that her son john would always look pale and plain beside the charming harry. But it didn't bother the two princes, and they became fast friends and loved one another like real brothers. The queen, however, was not content and she set off to find a way to spoil harry so john would be the best in the castle.

To that end, she sought the advice of an old woman who lived near the palace on a farm and was known to have magical powers. "So you say young harry is too charming for his good?" said the woman. "That is a simple enough problem to fix. Send him to me in the morning."

So early the next morning, the queen found harry and said, "Such a nice day! I believe I'll walk myself to the farm for this morning's eggs. Harry, be a dear and join me." So Prince Harry accompanied his stepmother, the queen. When they arrived at the woman's cottage, they knocked on the door. "How can I help you?" said the woman, who knew very well why the queen had come. Said harry, "We've come for some eggs for breakfast. Do you have any?" "Of course! Just come inside and get some eggs from that pot over there!" Harry lifted the lid off the pot, and at that moment a vicious black smoke blew out of the pot. As he inhaled the smoke he began to change. His face got misshaped, his ears grew pointy and enlarged and his body became weaker and thinner and his skin turned into a dull shade of green. The queen felt entirely satisfied and she returned home with poor Prince harry trailing behind, his head bowed low.

The servants at the palace were horrified at the terrible event that had befallen poor Prince harry. And none was more horrified than the queen's son, Prince John. "harry!" john said to his half-brother, "what shall we do?" he tried everything he could think of to get him to feel better, but he was too grieved and sickly. "How did this happen to you?" he cried. But whenever poor harry tried to tell john, nothing but strange sounds came from his mouth. "Well, we can't let you be seen like this," John decided. he took a fine cloth and wrapped it around his brother's head. "We must go and try to get help." john took his brother by the hand and they left the castle.

They went on, and they went on and on and on, till at last, they came to a castle. John knocked at the castle door and asked if he and his poor sick brother could stay the night. The servant who answered the door said that that would be impossible, as this was the home of a king who had two daughters, and the younger princess was sickening away to death, and no one could find out what was wrong with her, so they could not possibly entertain visitors that evening.

John begged the servant, saying that he of all people understood how terrible that can be because his brother was also quite sick. Besides, he and his brother were so very tired and so needed a place to spend the night. The servant sighed and disappeared for a while. When he returned he said that John and his brother could spend one night at the castle, but only on one condition. The servant explained that the curious thing about the illness of the young princess was that whoever watched her at night was never seen again. Now if john would agree to stay up with her and nurse her all night long, then he and his brother could stay the night. Added to that, the king would give him a bag of silver. John quickly agreed.

John and his brother were led to the princess' room, where they were both fed and made comfortable for the evening.

Soon poor harry was nodding and had fallen asleep by the fire. Till midnight all went well. As the midnight bells rang, however, the sick princess got up out of bed as if in a daze, dressed, and walked downstairs. John was surprised to see her rise and move. he followed her outside the castle and she didn't seem to notice him. The princess went into the stable where she saddled her horse, called her hound, and jumped into the saddle. john lightly leaped behind her on another horse to follow her. they rode and as they passed through the woods, john plucked apples from the trees to have in the morning, and he filled his leather pouch with them.

When they came to a hill, the princess spoke loudly: "Open, open, oh hill, and let me in". Immediately, a passage in the hill opened. At the end of the passage, the princess entered a magnificent hall, brightly lit up. Many beautiful fairies surrounded the princess and led her off to dance. Meanwhile, John, without being noticed, watched the princess dance and dance and dance until she fell, exhausted, on a couch. The fairies fanned her until she could rise, and dance again some more.

At the first ray of dawn, the bells rang, and the princess hastened to get back on her horse. John jumped up behind him on his horse and they rode for home. By the time the morning sun rose, the servants entered the princess's room. They were very surprised to discover john was still there! There sat the boy, sitting by the fire, eating apples. John said the princess had had a good night, and that he would gladly sit up with her again a second night, but for that, he must have a bag of gold.

The second night passed in much the same way. The princess rose at midnight and rode away to the hill and the fairy's ball, and John went with her, gathering apples as they rode through the forest. This time, he did not watch the princess as closely, for he knew what she would do -- dance and dance all night long with the fairies. Instead, he watched a fairy play with a wand. Then, he overheard one of the fairies say, "Three strokes of that wand would make john's sick brother as charming as he ever was." So john rolled apples to the fairy till the fairy set down the wand to crawl after the apples. Then john quickly picked up the wand and wrapped it in his coat. At dawn, he and the princess rode home as before.

When the castle servants came in the next morning, they again found john sitting at the fireside eating apples comfortably. "You are still here -- again!" they cried. Motioning to the Princess, asleep in her bed, they said, "Has the Princess had another good night?" "Yes, another good night," he said. As soon as the castle servants left, john removed the cloth that covered his brother's ugly head. With the fairy's wand, he touched his brother's head lightly three times. At once the nasty magic began to fly away and his skin changed back to normal, his ears and his face became regular, and harry was his charming self again. The two princes were both delighted. And so were the castle attendants, who noted that the sick brother had been cured, and what's more, that he was remarkably lovely to look at besides. Plus the princess seemed no worse, and the young boy hadn't disappeared for two nights straight. So john was asked to stay yet the third night with the princess. He agreed, but only if he could marry the sick princess.

Everything went on as on the first two nights. This time the fairy was playing with a basket of corn, and John heard one of the fairies say, "Three sips of corn soup would make the sick princess as well as he ever was." So john rolled a few apples he had gathered to the fairy, who left the basket of corn behind to chase after them. Then he reached into the basket and put a handful of corn into his leather pouch.

At dawn, they set off again, but instead of eating his apples as he had done before, this time john boiled the corn and made a pot of corn soup. Soon the room was filled with a very savory smell. "Oh!" said the sick princess, "could you please give me a sip of that corn soup." So john gave her a spoonful of the soup, and she rose on her elbow. She loved it and spoke again, "please give me another sip of that soup!" So john gave her another spoonful, and she sat up on her bed. Then she said again, "just a little more! please!" So john gave her a third spoonful, and she rose healthy and strong, completely cured. Then the princess dressed and sat down by the fire.

When the castle servants came into the princess's room the next morning, they were astonished to find the princess sitting beside john, and the two of them chatting away and happily eating apples by the fire. Meanwhile, the princess's sister had met harry in the castle byways and she had fallen in love with him, as nearly everybody did. Soon it was agreed that the two of them, too, should be married. And so the two princesses married the two princes, and all of them lived happily ever after.

THE MAGIC BEAR

"Once upon a time, there was a boy so poor that he had to wander around the country looking for work. One day a farmer hired him to watch his goats. So each day he would take his goats to the fields and bring them back at the end of the day.

One morning in the fields, the boy heard a scream that sounded almost human. he rushed to the spot. There, to his surprise, was a bear crying out in pain.

Though he was scared the boy drew nearer and saw that he had a large thorn in one foot. he carefully pulled out the thorn, bound up the wound with his handkerchief, and the bear licked his hand with his big rough tongue. Suddenly remembering his goats, the boy rushed back to the meadow. he searched everywhere but could not find even one goat. What could he do but to return home and confess to his master? He scolded him bitterly and, afterward, beat him. Then he said, "Tomorrow you will have to look after the sheep. Be sure you do not lose any of them!"

Exactly one year after he had found the bear, the boy was tending the sheep one morning when he again heard a groan which sounded quite human. And there was the same bear on the ground, this time with a deep wound across his face.

No longer afraid of the creature, he washed the wound, lay healing herbs on it, and bound it up. The bear thanked him as he had done before. Worried, he rushed back. But again, the sheep in her flock was gone! he searched everywhere, but it was no use.

He sank to the ground and wept bitterly, not daring to return to his master empty-handed. At last, he thought that if he climbed a tree he might get a wider view of the land and find his lost sheep. But no sooner was he seated on the highest branch that something happened which put the sheep quite out of his mind. Out of the woods walked a beautiful young girl who came to his tree. She moved aside a large rock by the tree trunk, stepped down into what looked like a deep black hole, and disappeared.

The boy was so curious that he decided to stay in the tree all night long until the young girl came out again. The next morning, the rock was moved aside, but the young girl did not come out, a bear came out instead. The bear looked around, then very slowly padded into the forest and disappeared from view.

Now the boy was so curious that he climbed down the tree to see the rock for himself. It seemed like an ordinary enough rock. Yet he easily pushed it aside and discovered a deep opening underneath. he carefully stepped down, found a track, and following a path was led to a beautiful house. In the house, he discovered a library, and there he passed hours reading very good books which had the best stories he had ever read and the best poems and left a favorite of his out on the table. Then he prepared a good dinner (eating a bit of it himself, as he was very hungry!), and climbed back up to the top of his tree. he looked again for his lost sheep, but not a trace of one could he see.

As the sunset, the same bear, walking much better this time, came out of the woods and back to the rock under the tree. Down he went and a while later, out came the same young girl. Again she looked about her left and right, saw no one, and softly stepped into the forest.

The boy came down from the tree and did what he had done the day before, each time leaving a different book on the table and preparing a meal before he left. Thus three days went by. The next time the young girl emerged, he called out, "Stop! Please, won't you tell me your name?"

The young girl, surprised, said, " you must be the one who's been setting out the books and preparing my dinner!" she explained that she was a princess. Years ago, she had been captured by an elf who cast a spell on her. All-day long she must be a bear. Only at night could she return to her human shape. As a bear, she had been the very one whom he had helped twice before. What's more, she whispered, the elf who had enchanted her was the very same one who had stolen his goats and his sheep, out of spite for the kindnesses he had shown to her, when she had been wounded as a bear.

The boy asked, "How can you be freed from the spell?"

"There is only one way," she said with a sigh, "and that is if someone can get a lock of hair from the head of a king's daughter, spin it, and from its cloth make a cloak for the elf."

"Then I will go at once to the king's palace," said the boy.

So, they parted. When the boy arrived at the king's palace he was careful to wash and neatly arrange his hair. Quickly he was hired as a kitchen helper. Soon everyone at the palace talked about his neat and clean appearance.

By and by the princess heard of him and sent for the boy. When she saw him, and how neatly he had dressed, the princess told him that he was to come and comb out hers.

Now the hair of the princess was very thick and shone like gold. The boy combed it and combed until it was brighter than the sun. The princess was pleased and invited him to come every day and comb her hair. At last, the boy took courage and asked permission to cut off one of the long, thick locks.

The princess, who was very proud of her hair, did not like the idea of parting with any of it, so she said no. But each day the boy begged to be allowed to cut off just one lock of her thick hair. At last, the princess gave in. "Very well then!" she finally exclaimed, "you may have it, on one condition -- that you find for me the finest storybook in all the land and bring it to me!"

The boy answered that he would do so, and he cut off the lock. When he was alone, he wove it into a cloak that glittered like silk. When he brought it to the young girl, she told her to carry it straight to the elf, who lived on top of a high mountain. But she warned him that he must announce loudly that he was bringing the cloak, or the elf would surely attack him.

Before the boy reached the top of the mountain, outrushed the elf, waving in one hand a sword and a club in the other. Quickly he called out that he had brought him a cloak. At that, the elf stopped and invited him into his house.

He tried on the cloak but it was too short. Angry, he threw it onto the floor. The boy picked up the cloak and quickly left. he returned quite an in despair to the king's palace.

The next morning, when he was combing the princess' hair, he begged and begged for permission to cut off just one more lock. At last, the princess gave in, on one condition - that the boy would find her another book with the best poems in the entire world.

The boy said softly that he had already found such a book for her. Later, the boy spun more thread from the second lock. Now he could lengthen the elf's cloak and sleeves. When it was finished, he carried it again to the elf. This time the cloak fits perfectly! The elf was quite pleased, and he asked him what he could do for him in return. he said that the only reward he could give him was to take the spell off the princess so she could stay human, night and day.

For a long time, the elf would not hear of reversing his spell, but he liked the cloak so well that at last, he said yes. He even told him the goats and sheep would be returned to his master by the end of the day. And this was the secret to freeing the princess of the magic - he must cast the bear into the pond near the mountain until he was entirely underwater. Then, when the princess finally emerged she would be free from the magic forever. The boy went away in despair, for fear that the elf was trying to trick him, and that after he had cast the bear into the water he would find that he had only drowned the princess.

At the bottom of the mountain, he joined the princess, who was waiting for him. When she heard his story she comforted him and bade him to be of good courage and to do as the elf had said. And so in the morning when she emerged in her bear form, the boy cast her into the pond near the mountain until she was entirely underwater. Soon after, out of the water came the princess, beautiful as the day, and as glad to look upon as the sun itself.

The young girl thanked the boy for all he had done for her and declared that she would like him to be her groom and no one else. They went together to the king's palace, where the princess with the golden hair lived. When the king and queen saw the young girl approach, a great joy filled their hearts. It was their youngest daughter! She had long ago been enchanted by an elf and had disappeared from the castle. Their daughter, the princess with the golden hair, was delighted to see her long-lost sister. The princess asked her parents' permission to marry the boy who had saved her. And so the boy and the princess were married, later became the rulers of the land, and over time they richly deserved all the honors showered upon them.

SUPERPOWERS

"Once again Robert lost count of the sparkly green stars glued to his ceiling and so he begins again for the third time. Just like every night, Robert was having trouble sleeping, the thought of spending 6 hours in a beige rectangular, industrial type building that was his school, horrified him. Don't get him wrong, he liked studying, he was a good student and an exquisite artist, he just didn't have friends.

Every day came with a new challenge, sometimes it was his bow tie that was made fun off and at other times it would be his big, round glasses that his mother thought made him look like a moon pie that he was. There was just something about Robbie that didn't draw people to him. Maybe it was his elderly outdated name, Robert or his painfully shy personality. Robbie silently suffered the mischievous acts of other children in school, it was the night that was hard, he felt lonely and sad. Just like other children he wanted to have friends so he could talk about his favorite comic book series, share his lunch, go to the ice-cream parlor and eat his most preferred blueberry ice-cream whilst discussing the new Avengers movie.

This night was somehow different, the air against his face felt colder than usual, he could sense the eeriness that hung heavily in his room. Normally something like this would scare him but it seemed nothing compared to the turmoil he faces in school so he closes his eyes in an attempt to sleep hoping that tomorrow would be a better day. The minute he closed his eyes, and oozing sound started encompassing the room, it was deafening, frightened Robbie was up in a split second calling out for his parents but he wasn't sure if they could hear him over the thunderous sound. With every second the noise seemed to be getting louder and louder and with it came a strong breeze, hard and cold. The terrified little boy curled up, closed his eyes and blocked his ears with his hands. The horror continued for eternity, something tapped against his bedroom window, shakenly Robbie peeked and saw a circular metallic object with shinning red and green light if Robbie's memory served him right, it seemed like a spaceship just like in The Lego part 2.

After what felt like an eternity, the noise and gushing air stopped, Robbie slowly removed his hands from his ears and opened his eyes as his trembling hands went in search for his glasses. With the side lamp illumining his small room, he saw something perking up from his window, he slowly made his way towards the window sill. Something moved and he instantly regretted his decision, running back to his bed. To his horror, a green ball-like thing uncoiled into a small creature with big round eyes, resembling Robbie's but what looked odd was his long antenna-like ears. Almost 2 feet tall, the little creature's puppy eyes looked up to Robbie's as if asking for help. His long branches of fingers intertwined with one another indicated he was scared.

Robbie jumped off the bed, maintaining his safe distance, he knelt even then they were not at the same level. Robbie's trembling voice muttered, "who are you?"

The little creature looked confused and remained silent, his big eyes still ogling Robbie.

"Where did you come from?" Robbie continued.

No response.

"I'm sorry, I am such a bad host, would you like something to eat?", Robbie didn't expect a response, rather it was a rhetorical question.

Robbie immediately left the room and tiptoed towards the kitchen. He poured a glass of milk and grabbed two cookies from "earn it" jar which he is awarded for good grades in tests.

Back in his bedroom, the green creature, still standing on the floor with his puppy eyes scanning the room.

"Do you like cookies?" Robbie inquired while handing him his treat.

The response was rather aggressive, he snatched the snack from Robbie's hand and it was gone in a split second. The look on his face was now of satisfaction and Robbie's of amusement.

They both sat together in silence but for some strange reason it was not awkward, it was comforting. Maybe Robbie found the friend he had been looking for.

Robbie doesn't remember going to bed and drifting off to sleep, the next morning when his mother woke him up for school he was perfectly tucked in his bed. Baffled, Robbie woke up rubbing his eyes believing it was a dream, it made him a little sad and disappointment took him over. Right after his mom left the room, he heard a thud from under his bed along with something that sounded like "ouch", the green creature stumbled out from under his bed rubbing his bead. A wide smile drew on Robbie's face, disappointment was replaced by happiness making him jump off the bed and hugging the strange creature that now apparently lives under his bed.

He was taken by surprise and was unresponsive for a few seconds before hugging him back. "Can I call you Liam?", Robbie asked. The sly smile on his face suggested he was okay with it.

Liam followed Robbie as got up to get ready, he watched him wash his face and brush his teeth, mimicking the same behavior, it made Robbie laugh. He was happy, truly happy.

"Liam, I have to go to school right now, will you be here when I come back so we can play with my brand new Lego?" Robbie asked, a little worried that he might leave him, something exchanged between the two new best friends assuring Robbie of Liam's presence on his return.

Nothing in school bothered him that day, he was happy and excited. Even Ted making fun of his clothes again didn't bother him, he was thrilled to go back home. As the bell during the last class rang, Robbie was the first one to pack up his things and leave for the home which was quite awkward for the whole class because Robbie never did that before. That day he didn't even stop to see the girl he liked from his art class, Gwen, for whom he'd wait for almost 10 minutes every day because she got off 10 minutes after Robbie.

Robbie reached home when the longer needle touched 2 along with the smaller needle. Robbie drifted through the hallway, ignoring his mother's greetings something he would never do even if the world was ending. Robbie was only thinking about his new green little "alien" best friend that he thought would've left. While running on the stairs, Robbie tripped over his open shoelace. His mom was watching all this.

Robbie thought it's the end, while his head was in the air. Robbie closed his eyes. At that very instinct ticking of the clock stopped, Robbie felt like time has stopped, his movement stopped. It was unrealistic. Robbie started to get tilted in the upright direction until he was standing on his feet. It was unbelievable. He saw Liam (green alien friend) standing at the door of his room. Then he looked at his mother, who he thought has seen everything and is going to go mad at what she just saw but to his shock, she was standing there still, paused. He realized that the clock needles weren't moving. Everything was still. He rushed towards his room. After he closed the door behind him, he listened heard the dishes in the kitchen falling and his mom shouting Robbie's name. Everything was back to normal except the gaze with which Robbie was looking at Liam. Now he knew that his new alien friend is no normal being but has superpowers. Robbie was jumping with excitement.

Liam gave out an 'alienating' smile as a reaction to Robbie's excitement. "TELL ME THIS ISN'T A DREAM! ARE WE FRIENDS? YES, YOU ARE MY FRIEND WITH SUPERPOWERS! YOU'LL HELP ME DO MY HOMEWORK, YOU'LL PLAY WITH ME, I HAVE THE COOLEST BEST FRIEND EVER YESSSS"! Robbie kept shouting until his mom knocked on the door. All of a sudden, Robbie went silent, the smile faded. A situation of distress was created in his mind because he didn't want to share this secret with his mother (as he believed that she'll report Liam to the security agencies because his mother was a strong believer that aliens will land and end this planet one day). Robbie panicked and stood in front of Liam while his mother entered the room with a weird smile on her face. "Honey is everything okay? I heard you shouting……". "Yes mom, everything's fine, I just found out something I lost a few days back," said Robbie, trying hard to not let Liam be seen. "What are you hiding behind your back Robbie? Move let me look at it, what is it"? Mom questioned. Robbie moved away slowly also turning his back at his mom. Liam was standing there wearing his innocent face. Robbie's Mom all shocked, stared at Robbie and did that 'what' gesture towards him. Before his mom could say anything, Robbie started to explain, "Mom I can explain, this is Liam……"

"Who? Where? Robbie are you okay?" Robbie's mom interrupted.

Robbie realized that his Mom isn't able to see Liam. He was relieved, didn't know or thought about the reason because everything going on was insane at that moment. Robbie somehow managed to cover up from there and send his mom out of the room.

"So let me get this clear, you have superpowers and only I can see you, how cool is that"? Robbie announced. Then he hugged his Liam, but all of a sudden he jumped back after he got an electric shock from its hands, but then Liam moved forward and held Robbie's hands and shake them well.

"Friend, you are a friend," said the alien. Robbie was completely shaken now. "I transferred your language into me by holding your hands, now I'm also able to speak friend," Liam said smiling.

Robbie never felt this lively his entire life. Liam was the first being, not human, but being who called Robbie a friend. Then Robbie took Liam along him outside his house to see what he could do. When Robbie asked Liam that why wasn't he visible to his mom, it replied, "I saw that face of yours, I knew you didn't want to expose me to your mom, that's why I went invisible for her." Then Liam explained to Robbie that he has come to this planet to meet Robbie and give him what was promised to his father on his birth. Robbie's father was a scientist who disappeared just after he was born. Liam told him that his father is their king, king of a whole planet with aliens and he has sent Liam with gifts which it is supposed to give to Robbie on his 10th birthday which was only two days from now. Until then Liam was to guide and tell Robbie what and how to use those powers. Robbie was excited, yet confused. They were walking down the street when they saw a thief snatch purse from a lady and run, she shouted for help but no one came because of the gun thief carried.

Liam said "Check this out" and ran with the speed of light, without touching the thief he threw the thief on the ground.

Everyone started to scream as they saw a green alien crawling on the street but this was all kind of relatively normal for Robbie. Liam panicked and again went visible. Robbie ran shouting towards the point where Liam was last seen shouting that it's okay, it's just a kid, but no one stopped running. Liam reappeared when Robbie came near him. They both vanished from there and ended up standing on a mountain. Robbie had no idea where they were, it was a mountainous area. Liam told Robbie that he cannot stay on Earth anymore because his cover is exposed to humans and it won't be safe for either Robbie or his family if Liam stayed there anymore. So Liam held Robbie's hands and closed his eyes. Robbie copied him. He felt as the current is flowing through his arms but it was a ticklish feeling. After a while, Robbie felt that Liam is not holding his hands anymore, when he opened his eyes, Liam was nowhere to be seen. Robbie was back at his place but something was strange about everything around him. Everything seemed smaller in size until he faced his mirror.

Robbie stood there shook, he was no more a 10-year-old kid. He was a 25-year-old guy wearing a red cape. He was not Robbie anymore. He had an S written on his chest. He was the superhero for whom the world was waiting for. He was the superman of this century.

THE GHOST OF THE PRINCE

"Long time ago there lived a very rich king with his queen and they had a wonderful baby boy together. The night before their son was born, the mother had a dream. She dreamt that the only way her son would reach adulthood would be if the child's feet never touched the earth until he was ten years old.

Great care was taken that this should be avoided, and only trustworthy nurses were hired to look after the child. As the years passed, he was always diligently guarded. Sometimes he was carried in his nurses' arms, sometimes the servants carried him in a chair, but the boy's feet never touched the ground. So it passed until the child was nearly ten years old.

When the child's tenth birthday drew near, the parents began to plan a magnificent feast to celebrate their son's release. One day while the preparations were in progress, a frightful noise, followed by most unearthly yells, shook the castle. In her terror, the queen dropped the child. At that very instant the noises stopped. On turning around to pick up the boy again, imagine her alarm when she found him no longer there! With a cry, she realized that she had doomed her son. The child's feet had touched the floor, and now the child was gone.

Hearing her screams and wails, all the servants of the castle ran to her. The father soon followed, asking, "What is the matter? What has happened? Where is our son?" The queen, trembling and weeping, told of the disappearance of their only child, and so soon before his tenth birthday.

No words can describe the anguish of the father's heart. He sent servants in every direction to hunt for the boy; he gave orders; he begged; he threw away money left and right; he promised everything, anything! if only his son might be brought back to him. The search was made immediately, but no trace of the boy could be found. He had vanished as completely as if he had never existed.

Many years later the unhappy king learned that in one of the most beautiful rooms of the castle, footsteps as if someone were walking up and down the halls, and dismal cries and groans, were heard each night at midnight. Anxious to follow up the matter, for he thought it might in some way give a clue as to the whereabouts of his lost son, he made known that a reward of three hundred gold pieces would be given to anyone who would watch for one entire night in the haunted room. Many were willing, but had not the courage to stay till the end; for at midnight, when they heard dismal groans and footsteps coming closer and closer, they would shriek and run away rather than risk their lives for three hundred pieces of gold. The poor father was in despair and knew not how to discover the truth of this dark mystery.

Now close to the castle there dwelt a widow, a miller by trade, who had three daughters. The family was very poor and hardly earned enough to meet their daily needs. When they heard of the midnight noises in the castle and the promised reward of 300 gold pieces, the eldest daughter said, "As we are so very poor, surely we have nothing to lose. We might try to earn these three hundred gold pieces by remaining in the room for one night. I should like to try, Mother, if you'll let me."

The mother hardly knew what to say. She was worried, of course, because she had heard of the terrible noises that had frightened so many others away. But when she thought of their poverty and the difficulty they had day to day in setting food on the table, she permitted her eldest daughter to remain one night in the haunted room. Then the daughter went to the castle to ask the king's consent.

"Do you have the courage to watch for a whole night in a room haunted by ghosts?" said the king, "Are you sure you are not afraid, my girl?"

"I am willing to try, and I can start this very night," said the eldest daughter. "I only ask you to give me some food to cook for my supper, for I am very hungry."

Orders were given that she should be supplied with everything she wanted, and indeed enough food was given to her, not for one supper only, but three. With the food, some dry firewood, and a candle she entered the room. She first lit the fire and put on her saucepans, then she laid the table and made the bed. This filled up the early part of the evening. The time passed so quickly that she was surprised to hear the clock strike twelve. At the last stroke, footsteps, as if of someone walking, shook the room, and dismal groans filled the air. The frightened girl ran from one corner to the other but could see no one. But the footsteps and the groans only got louder.

Suddenly a young man appeared. He approached her and asked, "For who is this food cooked?"

Startled, she said, "For me."

The gentle face of the stranger saddened. Then he asked, "And this table, for who is it laid?"

After a moment, she said again, "For me."

The brow of the young man clouded over and the beautiful blue eyes filled with tears as he asked once more, "And this fire, for who have you built it?"

"For myself," replied she.

Tears fell from his eyes as he waved his arms and vanished.

The next morning she told the nobleman all that had happened in the room but without mentioning the painful impression her answers seemed to make on the stranger. She gratefully received the three hundred golden crowns for having stayed the whole night in the haunted room. And the father was thankful to have at last heard something that might lead to the discovery of his son. On the following day, the second daughter, having been told by her sister what to expect and how to answer the stranger, went to the castle to offer her services and to earn another three hundred gold pieces. The king agreed, and she was provided with everything she might want. Without loss of time, she entered the room, lit the fire, put on the saucepans, spread a white cloth upon the table, made the bed, and waited for the hour of midnight. When the young stranger appeared and asked, "For who is this food prepared? for who is the table laid? for who is the fire built?" she answered as her sister had bidden her do: "For me, for myself only."

As on the night before, tears ran down his face, he waved his arms and disappeared.

The next morning, she told the nobleman all that had happened in the room except the sad impression her answers seemed to make upon the stranger. The three hundred gold pieces were given to her, and she went home.

On the third day, the youngest daughter wanted to try her fortune.

Now the widow dreaded to expose her youngest daughter to any danger, but as the two elder ones had succeeded in staying in the room and bringing home three hundred gold pieces, she allowed her to take a chance. So with the instructions from her two older sisters as to what she should expect and what she should say, and with the king's consent and abundant provisions, she entered the haunted room. Having lit the fire, put on the saucepans, laid the table, and made the bed, she waited with hope and fear for the midnight hour.

At midnight, the room was shaken by the footsteps of someone who walked up and down, and the air was filled with cries and groans. The girl looked everywhere, but no living being could she see. Suddenly there stood before her a young man. He pointed to the table and asked, "For who have you prepared this food?"

Now her sisters had told her exactly what to expect and what to say, but when she looked into the sad eyes of the stranger, she was confused and silent.

"Why don't you answer me: For who is the food prepared?" he asked impatiently. Somewhat confused, she stuttered, "I-I prepared it for me, but you, too, are welcome to it."

At these words, his brow grew more relaxed.

"And this table, for who is it spread?"

"For myself," said the girl. Then she added, "unless you will honor me by being my guest."

A smile brightened his face.

"And this fire, for who have you built it?"

"For myself, but you are welcome to sit by it with me."

He clapped his hands for joy and replied, "Ah, yes! that's right. I accept the invitation with pleasure. But please wait for me. I must first thank my kind friends for the care they have taken of me."

At that moment, a deep opening appeared in the middle of the floor. The youth descended into the hole. She, anxious to see what lay below the floor, followed him, holding on to his mantle. Thus they both reached the bottom.

Down below a new world opened itself before her eyes. To the right flowed a river of liquid gold; to the left rose high mountains of solid gold; in the center lay a large meadow covered with millions of flowers. The stranger went on; the girl behind him followed unnoticed. As he went, he saluted the field flowers as old friends. Then they came to a forest where the trees were all made of gold. Many birds flew around the young man, perching on his head and shoulders. While he spoke to and petted each one, the girl broke off a branch from one of the golden trees and hid it as a remembrance of this strange golden land.

Leaving the forest of gold, they reached a wood where all the trees were of silver. Animals of various kinds crowded around the youth. He spoke to each one and stroked and petted them. Meanwhile, the girl broke off a branch of silver from one of the trees.

When the young stranger had said good-bye to all his friends, he returned by the paths he had come. Arriving at the foot of the opening to the castle room, he began to rise, she coming silently after, holding on to his mantle. Up they went higher and higher until they reached the opening to the room in the castle. The floor closed up behind them without a trace. The girl returned to her place by the fire, where she was sitting when the young man approached.

"All my farewells have been spoken," he said. "Now we can have supper."

She hastened to place upon the table the food she had prepared before, and sitting side by side in front of the fire they supped together. When they had finished he said, "Now it is time to rest."

He lay down on the bed, and the girl placed by his side the gold and silver branches she had picked in the sparkling world below the floor. In a few moments, he was sleeping peacefully. She then settled comfortably in a soft chair beside him.

The next day the sun was already high in the sky, and yet the girl had not come out of the room to give an account of what had happened. The king became impatient, pacing the floor and worrying about what might have happened to the girl. At last, he determined to go and see for himself what had happened.

Picture his surprise and joy when on entering the haunted chamber he saw his long-lost son sleeping on the bed, while beside him sat the widow's beautiful youngest daughter. At that moment the son awoke. The father, overwhelmed with joy, summoned the attendants of the castle to rejoice.

BELLE AND THE PRINCE

"Once upon a time, in a town called Lycia, there lived a merchant who sold spices, and he had a daughter named Belle whom he dearly loved. Belle had a friend who was a fairy, and both Belle and her fairy friend were able to sing more sweetly and dance more gracefully than anyone else in the kingdom. For this reason, they were held in high favor by the king of fairyland. And the king's name was Ragnar. Belle had the loveliest hair in the world, for it was like spun gold, and the smell of it was like the smell of fresh roses. But her hair was so long and thick that the weight of it was often unbearable. One day she cut off a shining tress. Wrapping the hair in a large leaf, she threw it in the river which ran just below her window.

It so happened that the king's son was out hunting, and had gone down to the river to drink when there floated towards him a folded leaf, from which came a spice of roses. He opened it, and within he found a lock of hair like spun gold, and from which came a faint, exquisite fragrance. When the prince reached home that day he looked so sad and was so quiet that his father wondered if any ill had befallen him, and asked his son what was the matter. The prince took the tress of hair which he had found in the river. Holding it up to the light, he replied, "See, my father, was there ever hair like this? Unless I can win and marry the maiden that owns that lock of hair, I must die!"

So the king immediately sent heralds throughout all his dominions to search for the damsel with hair like spun gold. At last, he learned that she was the daughter of the spice merchant. Rumor spreads quickly. Soon Belle heard of this also. She said to her father, "If the hair is mine, and the king requires me to marry his son, then I must do so. But please ask the king to allow me this: that after the wedding, though I will stay all day at the palace, I wish every night to return to my old home."Her father listened to her with amazement, but answered nothing, as he knew she was wiser than him. Of course, the hair was Belle's, and soon the king summoned the spice merchant and told him that he wished for his daughter to be given in marriage to the prince.

The father bowed his head three times to the ground. He replied, "Your highness is our lord, and all that you bid us we will do. The maiden asks only this - that if, after the wedding, she stays all day at the palace, that she may be allowed to return each night to her father's house."The king thought this a very strange request but said to himself that it was, after all, his son's affair, and the girl would surely soon tire of going to and fro. So he made no difficulty, and everything was speedily arranged and the wedding was celebrated with great rejoicing.

At first, the condition attached to his wedding with the lovely Belle troubled the prince very little, for he thought that he would at least see his bride during the day. But to his dismay, he found that she would do nothing but sit the whole time upon a stool and he could never persuade her to say a single word. Each evening she was carried back to her house on a covered platform that was carried on poles on the shoulders of four men, a transport called a palanquin. Each morning, Belle returned soon after daybreak; and yet never a sound passed her lips, nor did she show by any sign all day long that she saw, or heard, or heeded her husband. Unhappy and troubled, the prince was wandering in an old and beautiful garden near the palace when he came upon the old gardener, who had served the prince's great grandfather. When the old gardener saw the prince he came and bowed before him and said, "Child! Why do you look so sad - what's the matter?"

The prince replied, "I am sad, old friend because I have married a wife as lovely as the stars, but she will not speak a single word to me, and I know not what to do. Night after night she leaves me for her father's house, and day after day she sits in mine as though turned to stone, and utters no word, whatever I may say or do."The gardener asked the prince to wait for him.

A little later he came back with five or six small packets, which he placed in the young man's hands. He said, "Tomorrow when your bride leaves the palace, sprinkle the powder from one of these packets upon your body. While continuing to see everything yourself, you will become invisible to everyone else. More I cannot do, but may all go well for you!"

The prince thanked him and put the packets carefully away in his turban. The next night, after Belle left for her father's house, the prince sprinkled the magic powder over himself, and then hurried after her. Indeed he was invisible to everyone else, although he felt as usual, and could see all that passed before him. He speedily caught up with the palanquin and walked beside it to the spice merchant's dwelling. There his bride entered the house. He followed silently behind her. Belle proceeded to her room where were set two large basins, one filled with rose oil spice and one of water. In these, she washed, and then she arrayed herself in a robe of silver, and wound about her neck strings of pearls, while a wreath of roses crowned her hair. When fully dressed, she seated herself upon a four-legged stool over which was a canopy with silken curtains. These she drew around her. Then she called out, "Fly, stool, fly!"

Instantly the stool rose in the air. The invisible prince, who had watched all these proceedings with great wonder, seized it by one leg as it flew away, and found himself being borne through the air at a rapid rate. In a short while, they arrived at the house of Belle's fairy friend, who, as I told you before, was also a favorite with the king of fairyland. The fairy stood waiting on the threshold, as beautifully dressed as Belle herself was. When the stool stopped at her door, the fairy friend cried in astonishment, "Why, the stool is flying all crooked today! I suspect that you have been talking to your husband, so it will not fly straight."But Belle declared she had not spoken one word to him, and she couldn't think why the stool flew as if weighed down at one side. The fairy looked doubtful, but made no answer, and took her seat beside Belle, the prince again holding tightly to one leg. Then the stool carried both on through the air until it came to the palace of Ragnar the king.

All through the night the women sang and danced before the king Ragnar, while a magic lute played by itself the most bewitching music the prince had ever heard, and the prince was quite entranced. Just before dawn, the king gave the signal to cease. Again the two women seated themselves on the stool and, with the prince clinging to one leg, flew back to earth, and bore Belle and her husband safely to the spice merchant's shop. Here the prince hurried straight on to the palace. As he passed the threshold of his rooms he became visible again. Then he lay down upon a couch and waited for Belle to arrive. As soon as she came, she took a seat and remained as silent as usual. For a while, not a sound was heard. Presently the prince said, "I dreamed a curious dream last night, and as it was all about you I am going to tell it to you."

The girl, indeed, did not respond to his words and stayed as still as ever. But despite that, he proceeded to relate every single thing he had seen the evening before, leaving out no detail. And when he praised her singing - and his voice shook a little - Belle just looked at him, but she said nothing, though, in her mind, she was filled with wonder."What a dream!" she thought. "Could it have been a dream? How could he have learned in a dream all I have done?" Still, she kept silent. Only she looked that one time at the prince and then remained all day as before.

When night came, the prince again made himself invisible and followed her. The same things happened again as had happened before, but Belle sang better than ever. In the morning the prince a second time told Belle all that she had done, pretending that he had dreamed of it. Directly after he had finished Belle gazed at him. She said, "Is it true that you dreamt this, or were you there?"

"I was there," answered the prince.

"But why do you follow me?" asked the girl.

"Because," replied the prince, "I love you, and to be with you is happiness."

This time Belle's eyelids quivered but she said no more and was silent the rest of the day. However, in the evening, just as she was stepping into her palanquin, she said to the prince, "If you do love me, prove it by not following me tonight."

And so, the prince did as she wished, and he stayed at home.

That evening when she and her fairy friend flew through the air on the magic stool, it flew so unsteadily that they could hardly keep their seats. At last, the fairy exclaimed, "There is only one reason that it should jerk like this! You must have been talking to your husband!" And Belle replied, "Yes, I have spoken!" But no more would she say.

That night Belle sang so marvelously that at the end, king Ragnar rose and vowed that she might ask whatever she liked and he would give it to her. At first, she was silent. But when he pressed her, she said, "If you insist, then I request the magic flute."The king, when he heard this, was displeased with himself for having made so rash a promise, because he valued the magic flute that played by itself above all his possessions. But as he had promised, so he must perform."You must never come back again," he said roughly, "for once having asked so much, how will you in the future be content with smaller gifts?"Belle bowed her head silently as she took the lute. She passed with the fairy out of the great gate, where the stool awaited them. More unsteadily than ever, it flew back to earth. When Belle got to the palace that morning she asked the prince whether he had dreamed again. He laughed with happiness, for this time she had spoken to him of her own free will. He replied, "No, but I begin to dream now - not of what has happened in the past, but of what may happen in the future."

That day Belle sat very quietly, but she answered the prince when he spoke to her. And when evening fell, and with it the time for her departure, she still sat on. The prince came close to her and said softly, "Are you not going back to your house tonight, Belle?"At that she rose and threw herself into his arms, whispering, "I will never leave you again!"So the prince won his beautiful bride.

THE WHITE WOLF

"Long ago, in a town near the Bluepeak Mountains in Pandora, there lived a young princess. Her mother, the queen, had been missing since she was a baby, and the princess knew very well the reason why. An enormous White wolf still lived in the Bluepeak Mountains who had tormented the town for years, coming down to prey not only on horses and cattle but even on the human beings who lived there. Years ago, her mother, who had been the finest hunter and gunman in the land, ventured into the Bluepeak Mountains to shoot the White wolf and to save the town. She had never returned.

When the princess was still small she already decided deep in her heart that when she grew up, she would be the one to shoot down the wolf that had overpowered her mother. As soon as she was allowed, she trained rigorously with the gun and became almost as good a gunman as her mother had been.

When she was fifteen years old, the princess went to her father and said, "father, I'm ready now to set out for the Bluepeak Mountains to find the White Wolf and defeat him. Please, let me go."

The king did not want to lose his daughter, too. With tears in his eyes, he said, "Even a famous marksman like your mother was lost to the terrible White Wolf. Please, sweetheart, quit dreaming about such nonsense and stay safe here at home."

"Don't worry, Father," the princess cried. "I shall find the White Wolf, I know it!"

Finally, the father said, "Very well, as you wish. But first, let me ask you one thing. Your mother used to have me stand with a water jug on my head. Then she would shoot off the handle of the water jug from one mile away without spilling any water. Can you do the same thing?"

When she heard this, the young princess immediately tried to match her mother's skill. She had her father stand one whole mile away, with a water jug on top of his head. She took careful aim but missed it. So she gave up her idea of going to the mountains and instead, practiced three more years with the gun.

After three years, she tried again. This time she succeeded in knocking off the handle of the water jug on her father's head without spilling a drop of water. Then the father said, "Actually, your mother was able to shoot the eye out of a needle from one mile away. Can you do this?"

The princess asked her father to place a needle in a tree trunk. Then she walked back for one mile. Taking careful aim, she let go of a shot but missed. Once again, she gave up the idea of going to the Bluepeak Mountains and settled down to another three years of practicing even harder. At the end of three years, she was 21 years old by that time, she again tried the same trick. This time, with the crack of her gun, the eye of the needle fell to the ground.

Now in fact, what the father had told his daughter about the amazing feats his mother used to be able to do, were all lies. The father had thought that if he told her impossible tales about the mother, the girl might give up her crazy idea of seeking the terrible White Wolf. But now that she had succeeded in performing each of the feats he told her his wife could do, the father could not help being impressed with her determination. So he permitted her to leave for the Bluepeak Mountains.

The princess was thrilled. She immediately set out. At the foothills, she came across a small inn. An old woman, who was the innkeeper, asked the young princess why she had come. She told her that her mother had been a victim of the White Wolf years ago and that she had practiced for many years to avenge her death.

The old innkeeper then said, "Ah, yes, I knew your mother. She was the greatest gunman in all the land. Why, she stopped here at this very inn, many years ago, before venturing into the Bluepeak Mountains. Can you see that tall tree over there in the distance? Why your mother used to turn her back to that tree and then shoot down the highest leaf on the highest branch from over her shoulder. If you can't do the same thing, how can you expect to defeat the White Wolf?"

The hunter's daughter, when she heard this, said she also would try. She placed her gun over her shoulder and took aim and shot. But she missed it. She knew then that she still wasn't ready, and she asked the old innkeeper to let her stay with her a while. From that day, she kept practicing shooting over her shoulder at the tree. After three more years, she was finally able to shoot down the highest leaf on the highest branch.

The old innkeeper told the hunter's daughter, "Just because you can do that, it still doesn't mean you can outshoot your mother. Why, your mother used to set an ant on the side of a cliff and then, from a distance of three miles away, she would shoot that ant off without even scratching the surface of the cliff. No matter what a fine gunman you may be, certainly, you can't match that."

The young princess, then, tried to do what the old innkeeper said her mother had done. Again she failed at first and had to practice three more years. Like her father, it turns out that all that the old innkeeper had told her had been made up because she, too, only wanted to save her life. But the princess, not questioning her once, had practiced until she could do the tasks she said her mother had done. The old innkeeper was filled with amazement.

"With your skill now, surely you will avenge your mother's death." So saying, the old innkeeper prepared a bag with many rice balls for her to eat along the way. The princess thanked her and started along the path leading into the heart of the Blue peak Mountains.

The young princess pressed deeper and deeper into the mountains. For days and days, she wandered through the wilderness. After all, the Bluepeak Mountains have twelve thousand peaks and stretch over a vast area, and she had no means of knowing just where the White Wolf was hidden. So she wandered on through the vast mountain ranges.

One day, while the princess was seated on a big rock nibbling a rice ball, a ragged old woman stumbled up to her and said, "Excuse me, miss. Could you spare an extra rice ball for me?"The daughter handed the old woman several rice-balls, which she ate ravenously. Then the old woman said, "We don't see many strangers this deep into these mountains. What brings you here?"

When the princess explained, the old woman shook her head vigorously from side to side. "Nay, good fellow," she said. "Forget about shooting the terrible White Wolf. He is too quick. As soon as the wolf desires to pounce, his next prey is gone.

From one day to the next, we never know whether we are going to survive to see the morrow. You are a young girl. You ought best to leave these mountains at once and go back home while you're still alive!" Then the princess replied that no, she would not be persuaded to leave. She described how hard she had practiced for so many years, and that now, with her skill, she knew she could smite the White Wolf after all. "Well," sighed the old woman, "if you are so sure, then you should know that the only way to shoot the White Wolf is to shoot him when all you see is but a white dot on the horizon. If you wait a single moment too late," here she shook her finger, "or if you miss your first shot, believe me, all will be lost for you."

The old woman left. The princess immediately took to scanning the horizon until she was entirely familiar with every curve and shadow on each mountainside far and wide. Thus she waited for hours, her gun at readiness. While the sun was setting, a single white dot appeared in a fraction of a moment on a distant mountainside. No dot had been there the moment before, the princess was certain of that. Instantly, she fired at the white dot. Her heart pounding, she raced toward the mountainside where she had aimed her shot.

And there she came upon the fallen White Wolf, nearly as big as a mountain itself. It had collapsed with its mouth open, ready to swallow its next prey -- her! Astonished by its size and thrilled that she had defeated the legendary beast, the princess stepped into the dead wolf's throat. Inside the wolf's mouth, she followed a black tunnel. Eventually, she came to a vast room as large as a fairground. This was the giant White Wolf's stomach.

The princess came upon an unconscious prince who lay huddled in a heap. The princess took the prince in her arms and nursed him until he awakened. The prince looked into her face and thanked her with all of his heart. he then revealed that he was the son of the king's highest advisor, who was famous in the capital city. The young prince told her how just the night before, the great White Wolf had stolen him away while he was practicing his bow outside on the veranda of his home.

Suddenly, the two of them heard a voice that sounded like a human. Puzzled, they groped in the dark toward it. When The voice belonged to an old woman crouched in the corner. Who was it but none other than the Queen! She had survived all these years inside the White Wolf's stomach on the prey swallowed by the great beast. The mother and daughter rejoiced in having found one another at last. Then together with the young prince, the three of them escaped through the wolf's mouth and found that they were in the middle of a large field. The young princess skinned a portion of the wolf, for she wanted to take home as a remembrance of the beautiful white wolf-skin. Taking the young prince by one hand and his father by the other, she proudly returned home, where her father was waiting for her. Words cannot describe his joy to see not only his son come safely back home, but his long lost wife, too!

The young hunter took the prince to his home in the capital city. His father cried tears of joy to see his son returning safe and sound. In gratitude, his father welcomed the young princess into his family to become his son's wife.

OUTCOME OF HARDWORK

"Once upon a time, there lived a shepherd, Samuel. He lost his father who was killed in a battle while Samuel was a baby. knight Jeremy. People used to call him, King of the Knights because he was the best. He led many wars and never lost. He was a celebrity in his kingdom and because of all this, his ego touched skies. He never talked to his father in public who was a blacksmith because he thought it'll affect his popularity. His father still prayed for the goodwill of his son and never showed how hurt he gets from his behavior. Jeremy's only mission now was to get married to the princess Carla. He thought because the King has high regard for him in his heart, it'll be easy for him to get married to the princess who was the only daughter of the King. King had no son so this made princess the heir to the throne and that's why it was an important and difficult task for the King to marry his daughter because whoever was going to marry her was eventually going to get the throne after him. Knight was unaware of the fact that Princess Carla was in love with some other guy. That guy was Samuel, an orphan with whom Carla was friends within their childhood because Samuel's mom used to work as a maid for Carla and

95

babysit her as Carla's mother passed away while giving birth to her. While Samuel's mother worked, Samuel and Carla used to play in the garden and as they grew old, they started to grow feelings for each other too. The problem was that they never confessed to each other.

Carla, being the daughter of a King, was a down to earth person. When Carla turned 20, King got a disease and he was told that he might not live for more than 2 months. He got worried about his kingdom and his daughter because he was aware of the fact that his daughter had no one to protect her and guide her fairly as she was too innocent. The next day he announced that a fest will be held 15 days from now on which competition will take place, whoever will win it is going to get married to the princess. This did offend the princess because she always dreamt that her father is going to ask her before deciding anything about her future. It was difficult but somehow King managed to explain the situation to his daughter without telling her about his disease.

Samuel got to know about the competition later that day, he went straight to Carla so he could tell her his feelings because he thought Carla will agree to run away with him and abandon her kingdom. Carla knew she can't face Samuel that's why she sent a message to him that either win this competition or forget her. Samuel was afraid of losing her but he was also aware that he cannot beat Jeremy or any other knight in sword combat or any other competition. Samuel worked as a normal shepherd and didn't know anything about fighting but his body was like a wrestler, strongly built. He was sad and went back to his place thinking of how he's never going to meet Carla again. This broke his heart. Samuel shared all this with an old man whom he met on his way the next day while he was grazing his flock. The old man was a wise man. He advised Samuel that he should not waste the next 15 days and should practice, at least he should give it a try otherwise he'll regret not doing it his whole life. The old man told him that it's better to try and lose rather than not trying and regretting it later. Adrenaline rushed through Samuel's veins. Now the only problem he was facing was that he didn't have anyone who'd teach him how to use a sword. The old man got up and promised him that he's going to teach him how to fight and everything else which he needs to win this competition. Samuel smirked and sat taking it as a joke because of how old man looked. The old man told Samuel that he was also a retired knight and was also the best one of his time but Samuel didn't believe it, so the old man took him to his place and showed him his sword which the same King gifted him when an old man saved his life 20 years back. Now Samuel started to trust the old man because he had no other choice.

Thirteen days were left until the day of the competition. The old man met Samuel at the place they decided to meet at and practice. It was still dark. The old man brought two thick sticks with him when Samuel asked what were they for, he replied, 'Young man, you don't want me to cut you into half on the very first day of the practice, do you"? This made Samuel laughed because he still thought that the old man was too weak to fight him now. The old man handed him over the stick and asked him to show whatever he can do with it. Samuel tried his best to hit old man and make him drop his stick he ended up losing his stick. He realized that this old man is going to train him well. Then the old man told Samuel to take 8 rounds of the ground they were training in. It was a huge ground where people used to run their horses. Samuel laughed and ignored it because according to him no one could do that. The old man kicked Samuel real hard while he was sitting on the rock, that Samuel rolled off. Samuel was shocked at the strength of the old man's kick. The old man said: I'm 70 years old son, I still have this much strength left in me because I used to take 8 rounds of this ground daily, that's why no one was ever able to beat me until I got retired. This is the key to your strength and stamina my son." Samuel all impressed looked at the ground and started jogging. Samuel hardly took 1 round and was going to faint, so the old man looking at his condition told him to take some rest. When

Samuel was about to sit, the old man stroked hard with his stick, Samuel didn't saw that coming and it hit on Samuel's thigh hard. Samuel cursed the old man while he got another stroke on his shoulder. Somehow he managed to defend his self from 5th and 6th attack of the old man. The old man said, "Samuel, if I was having a sword right now, I would have cut you down like a butcher cuts a goat, you need to sharpen your reflexes" Samuel when thought about the way old man attacked on him, he realized that this was the common attack any knight is going to do and he was impressed.

From that moment, Samuel started to do everything which old man told him to do because he realized if he has to win he has to work hard. On the other hand, the famous knight Jeremy was only focusing on eating and resting because he thought no one can ever beat him. 10 knight has had registered until now, and no one thought that any normal man will register for it until Samuel showed up. Jeremy laughed when he saw Samuel there. Samuel looked like a kid in front of Jeremy but Samuel was still confident enough to walk through all the Knights. King still didn't reveal what was going to happen in the competition other than fighting. It was going to be a surprise, he said.

Five days were left, Samuel and the old man were training again in the same place. Now Samuel was able to take 6 rounds of that ground and was able to tackle every attack from the old man. The old man was impressed but he still thought Samuel lacked some skills so he took him to a mountain. The old man said "Samuel, my son, you are now able to tackle my every attack, you've got much better stamina now but this isn't enough to pass the King's test. I've served this King for 15 years, Samuel, he is a wise man and is going to choose a wise man for his daughter too. I know you're a wise human but you also love the princess, you may lose your wisdom once you start to obsess over something my son. I hope you understand what I am trying to say, Samuel." The old man taught Samuel how to meditate, how to get into your true self without losing his wisdom. Samuel didn't know what benefit he's going to get out of all this but he did trust old man.

Finally, the sun of the most awaited day was up. 10 knights were in the arena, wearing their armor and Samuel was standing there too with his torn clothes. The arena was filled with an energetic crowd. The old man was also present in the crowd watching his student. Rules were announced loud and clear. Rules stated that all the participants are going to fight together, whoever loses their sword will be out of the competition, whoever enters the arena is going to be on their own and would be responsible for their selves. Samuel was a little bit scared, adrenaline was running through his vessels, his pupils were wide, on the other hand, Jeremy was feeling lazy and dizzy because his attitude made him think that he didn't need to exercise or practice anything.

Mediator shot his gun, starting the competition. All the Knights thought that taking Jeremy out first will make it easier for them to win in the end. Jeremy was the best one out of all others. Samuel analyzed the situation and thought it'd be better if he stays away for the time being. Another knight saw him standing at the side while all of them were fighting, 3 of them already lost their swords and had cut over their body too. A knight ran towards Samuel. Samuel knew how a knight attacks when he charges towards you so he tackled it smoothly which caused the knight to lose his sword. The crowd went silent. Everyone stopped because it wasn't normal for a normal boy to beat a knight in a single attack. Even Jeremy was shaking for a second. Jeremy took out other knights too in no time. He charged towards Samuel, but this time it was a different type of attack. Samuel almost lost his sword but thanks to the firm grip the sword had, he somehow managed to keep it in his hands. King stood up when he looked upon Samuel's sword closely. He realized it was the same sword he gifted to his life savior 20 years back. King smiled. The fight was stopped and rules for the last two contestants were revised. It was announced that now that you'll have to kill the other contestant to be declared as the winner and the drop of sword won't matter now. It was a one on one. Jeremy smirked as he moved towards Samuel. Samuel looked towards the old man, for guidance. Old man rotated his fingers clockwise and then anticlockwise, trying to tell him something. Samuel didn't understand but then he figured it out. The old man used to make Samuel run 8 rounds of that ground for a reason. Samuel realized that Jeremy had a huge body and he won't be able to run behind him for a long time. Samuel started to run clockwise, Jeremy laughed and started to run behind him charging with full force. Samuel took a break, dodged Jeremy's charge and started to run anticlockwise. He ran for 10 minutes with Jeremy on his back. Jeremy was out of form, he was already lazy so he started to feel dizzy. Samuel took his chance and charged towards Jeremy. He stroked Jeremy with the butt of his sword which caused Jeremy to fell on the ground and faint for a while.

Samuel stood on Jeremy, holding a sword in his hand, he looked at the King for him to grant him permission for this "murder".

King shouted, 'Granted' and the crowd went mad shouting, kill him.

Samuel looked at the Old Man. The old man smiled and closed his eyes and placed his hand on his heart, telling Samuel that do what your heart says, be yourself and not what people here want you to be, that is wisdom and that's something you won't regret about later. Samuel threw his sword away and announced Jeremy his mercy. Everyone went silent for a while but then started to shout, coward. Samuel turned his back and was about to leave because he thought he has lost it but then King stood up and said, "Oh you boy who carries wisdom and the sword of the man who saved my life once, I order you to come and receive your reward as you have not only won this competition but also my heart today".

Jeremy ran out of the arena that day and was never found. Samuel got married to princess Carla, they both laughed at the fact that they both loved each other but never confessed it. Samuel became king after the King died due to that disease. Samuel asked the old man to become his advisor because he thought he'll need his help but the old man replied, "Samuel, I'm here if you need any advice but it isn't thought to be a respectable thing to do if a retired knight takes on any other duty in his life later" and he refused the offer respectably.

The moral of the story is, hard work always pays off, ego leads you nowhere and is yourself, do what your heart says because you won't get more wise advice than what your heart says.

OLIVER AND THE
EVIL WITCH

"Once there was an evil witch who made a glass pot with her dark magic. If anyone would look at themselves in the water inside the pot the reflection that showed back was only dull and colorless.

The witch laughed. She wanted to show her evil pot to the whole world! She took it and flew up high on her broom. She flew so fast that the pot started to shake. She could no longer hold on to it and the pot dropped! It smashed into many tiny sharp bits of glass on the ground.

The wind blew the glass all over the place. From then on, if one bit of that evil glass blew into anyone's eye, that person would see only the bad and dark in people, no more the good. So it was in that land.

Years later, a boy named Oliver and a girl named Jenny were friends. They lived next door to each other. Both of them had their bedrooms in the attic. When they opened their attic windows, they were so close they could reach out and touch fingers. An old stream ran between the two houses. In the stream where water ran through, the families had planted a garden with vegetables and roses. It was like Oliver and Jenny's very own garden. Oliver and Jenny's families were poor. There were no toys to play with. But they did not mind. They played in their garden and were happy.

One day, Jenny and Oliver were weeding the garden. All of a sudden, a gust of wind blew by. It blew a sharp bit of that evil glass right into Oliver's eye. He stood up, stepping on the roses. "I do not want to weed this stupid garden anymore!" he said. "Okay," said Jenny. "Do you know you're stepping on the roses? How about a clapping game?"But Oliver cried out, "I don't care if I step on all the roses! And I never want to play with you, Jenny. Ever again!"

The next day, Oliver took his sled into town. Ah, that sled was so slow! A big white sleigh was coming down the road very fast. The sleigh came close to Oliver and as it did, it slowed down just a bit. Oliver had an idea. He quickly tied the rope of his sled onto the back of the sleigh. Now he could ride behind on his sled! But what Oliver did not know is that driving the sleigh was the evil Witch. The Witch, in her white fur coat, had known very well that Oliver was on the road. She had slowed down her sleigh when she got closer, to give him a chance to tie on the rope. She did not turn around to look. She knew that Oliver was speeding along behind her. Soon he would be near frozen with cold. Then, she knew, it would be easy to make him hers. The Witch drove on. When she knew Oliver must be bitter cold, she stopped the sleigh. She went up to the boy. "You want to ride behind my big sleigh?" said the Witch. "I can make it so you do not feel the cold." Oliver shivered. "I will give you one kiss on your cheek. Then you will no longer feel cold." Oliver nodded. She kissed him on the cheek. He no longer felt cold.

"Now, one more kiss," said the Witch. "With this one, you will forget all about Jenny and your family." Before Oliver could say anything, the Witch had kissed the other cheek. She laughed and said, "If I kissed you a third time on your forehead, you would die. But I have things for you to do for me back to my palace." Then she got into her sleigh and drove on.

Oliver did not return home that day. Or the day after that. You can imagine how upset everyone was! They said poor Oliver must have drowned in the river. Jenny ran down to the river. She called out to the waters rushing by - Is it true? The river would not say. Jenny took off her red shoes and held them up. She said she would throw her red shoes into the river if only the river would give back Oliver. But the river would not let her throw in the shoes. And that is how Jenny knew that he must not be under the water. But where was he?

Jenny went to many places looking for Oliver. She went to see a wizard. The wizard tried to trick Jenny into staying with him forever. Jenny ran out very fast, just in time. Then she met an old merchant. The merchant told Jenny that to find Oliver, she must go to the palace of a Princess. So off went Jenny to the palace of the Princess. He did not know anything about Oliver. But he gave Jenny warm clothes and a beautiful coach she could ride on her way.

Jenny was riding her coach when a band of robbers jumped up from behind. The robbers were led by Emma. Emma made Jenny go into the back of the coach. Then she took the reins. And Jenny was her prisoner! Poor Jenny! She had lost her coach. She was a prisoner. And she had no more clue than ever where to find Oliver. Emma took Jenny back to the house where she lived. Jenny must sleep in the barn, in a corner next to a horse.

When Emma had left, Jenny cried out, "Oh Oliver, where are you?" Two sparrows up high in the loft of the barn, heard her cry. Said one sparrow to her, "We remember seeing that boy Oliver you speak of." "You do?" said Jenny.

"What a sad day that was!" said the other sparrow. "That was when the Witch drove by on her sleigh. The boy Oliver was riding behind on his sled, very fast." "We were sitting in our nest," said the first sparrow. "When that evil Witch passed by, she turned and breathed on us." The sparrow could not finish, and the other one said, "Only my brother and I lived after that!"

"How terrible! I am so sorry for you," said Jenny. "But you saw my dear Oliver? Where was the sleigh headed? "Most likely the Witch was going to her palace in Land of frost," said the first sparrow. "That's where there are snow and ice all year long." "How will I ever find this place, Land of frost?" said Jenny. Then the horse, who was roped to a post, spoke up. "I know all about Land of frost," said the horse. "It is where I was born." "Please, could you take me there?" said Jenny. "Yes, I could, if only you and I were free of this place. But who knows how long we must stay here?"

Emma was just outside the barn door all this time. She was not so mean after all. She went into the barn and cut the ropes that bound the horse. She helped Jenny mount the horse and gave her a cushion to sit on. She even gave Jenny a pair of fur boots, two loaves of bread and a piece of bacon, too.

"Be off now," said Emma, "Find your friend."

Off like the wind flew Jenny and the horse. They rode and rode until it got dark. Then they needed to find a place to stay for the night.

They knocked on the door of a hut. An old woman opened the door and welcomed them in. Jenny and the horse told her about their search to find Oliver. The old woman said, "You still have a long way to go to get to Land of frost. The Witch's palace is 200 miles away."

"How will we find it?" said Jenny.

"The windows of her palace burn with a red light that can be seen for miles around," said she. "You can't miss it. But when you get there, do not go right up to the palace. First, look for a house nearby with a red door. Inside that house lives a Land of frost woman I know." The old woman picked up a piece of dried cloth and wrote some words on it. "Give her this cloth," said the old woman," and she will help you."

The next day, the horse and Jenny rode as fast as they could. They flew like the wind for three days. On the third day, they saw red lights from afar. When they got closer, they saw it was a large, dark palace, Nearby, just as the old woman had said, was a house with a red door. Very cold they were by then, and hungry too. And glad when a Land of frost woman opened the door and let them warm themselves by her fire.

Jenny told her that they had come looking for her dear friend Oliver. And that Oliver was last seen with the Witch. She handed the cloth to the Land of frost woman.

She read the words on the cloth three times. Then she put it in the pot on the fire for soup, as she never wanted to waste anything.

"Did it tell you anything at all?" cried out Jenny.

The horse said, "Something to give Jenny the power of ten men?"

"The power of ten men!" said the Land of frost woman, in a huff. "That would be of very little use. There is nothing anyone can do for this girl that she cannot do for herself!" She turned to Jenny. "Your friend Oliver got some bad glass in his eye. That is why the Witch took him. By now, she has probably kissed him twice. That gives her full power over him."

"Surely something can be done!" cried Jenny.

"Maybe," said the Land of frost woman. She turned to the horse. "Take Jenny to the Witch's palace. You will see a bush with red berries half covered in snow. Put her down at the bush and wait for her there while she goes to find Oliver. And Jenny," said she, turning to the girl, "there is something you must know. When you find Oliver, he will not want to leave. He is in her power. He thinks that her palace is the very best place in the world. He has forgotten all about you."

"What will I do?" Jenny cried out.

"Look at what you have already done!" said the Land of frost woman, "Look at how far you have already come."

And so, Jenny mounted the horse, and off they went. "Oh, no!" said Jenny after the house was no longer in sight. "I left my fur boots behind!" But there was no time to go back. So on they went.

At the bush with red berries, Jenny climbed off the horse. There she was, with no boots and her feet bare in the cold snow. But the Witch's palace was right ahead of her, its red lights burning in the windows. So Jenny walked on.

As she went, she called and called for Oliver. At last, there he was! He was sitting on top of a frozen lake, down on his knees. A throne sat on the lake, and it was empty the throne was the very throne of the Witch. "Oliver!" called Jenny. But he did not lookup.

Oliver's skin was dark blue as if he was frozen. He had so little feeling left he did not even notice the cold anymore. The Witch was away and Oliver was busy with his task, working on the frozen lake. He moved one piece of ice here and another there, making the words and numbers."Oliver!" called Jenny again. Still, Oliver did not lookup. Jenny ran right up to his face. "Oliver! Oliver!"

At last, Oliver looked up. But he looked right past her with his deep dark eyes and did not see her at all. Jenny burst into tears. Cold and cutting was the wind on that lake. As Jenny cried "Oliver, where are you?" one of her tears blew right onto Oliver's face. The tear burned his face until his whole face felt hot. Then Oliver, too, was crying.

"Jenny!" said Oliver, "is that you?" Oliver shivered. He cried with joy, for the evil bit of glass was washed from his eye. Oliver took Jenny's hands. Though they were both frozen cold, each of them felt warm inside. Jenny and Oliver walked hand in hand back to the bush with the red berries, where the horse waited. As they walked, the sun came out and warmed and dried them. The wind stopped and birds started to chirp. Before they knew it, there was a horse, in front of them. The horse took them back to the first old woman, who gave Jenny a new pair of fur boots. Each of them got a fur hat, too. As the horse carried them on the long road back home, who came along the road but Emma! She was riding the coach she had taken from Jenny, but Jenny was glad to see her, just the same. Emma said to Jenny, "So this is the friend you traveled across the world to save. I hope he was worth it!" They all smiled.

Emma said, "they should hop on her sleigh and she would give them a lift home."

By the time they finally got home, it was summertime. Much to their surprise, they were all grown up. In the years that came to be, Jenny and Oliver stayed the best of friends. There were no more adventures with the Witch or the cold frozen north, and each lived a quiet life. But they knew deep down that no matter what, they would always look out for each other.

PRINCE EDWARD AND THE BRACELET

"Once upon a time in the magical land of Islo, ruled a good and just king whose name was Arthur. The good king Arthur, knowing that he was dying, asked one last favor of his guardian pixie. He summoned the pixie and told her that he wanted to make this request on behalf of his son, Prince Edward.

"Say the word," answered the Pixie, "I will bestow any blessing upon your son, choose whatever you like for him."

"Ah," replied the good King, "It would do him no good to be rich, or handsome, or to possess all the kingdoms of the world if he were unhappy. You know very well that only a good man can be content. Madam, if you promised me to become his friend then, I know he would grow to be the best of princes."

"I will gladly become his friend," answered the Pixie; "But, it is not in my power to make Prince Edward a good man unless he will help me. He must himself try hard to become good. I can only promise to give him good advice, to scold him for his faults, and to punish him if he will not correct and punish himself."

The good King was satisfied with this promise. Very soon afterward he died.

Two days later, after the Prince had gone to bed, the Pixie suddenly appeared to him. She said, "I promised your father that I would be your friend, and to keep my word I have brought you a present." Then she put upon his wrist a silver bracelet."Take great care of this bracelet," she said: "it is more precious than diamonds. Every time you do a bad deed it will prick your wrist. If despite its pricking, you go on in your evil way, you will lose my friendship, and I shall become your enemy."

So saying, the Pixie disappeared, leaving Prince Edward very much astonished. For some time he behaved so well that the bracelet never pricked him. His subjects called him Prince Edward the Happy. One day, however, he went out hunting but could get no sport, which put him in a bad temper. It seemed to him as he rode along that his bracelet was pressing into his wrist, but as it did not prick him he did not heed it. When he got home and went to his room, his little dog Gogo ran to meet him, jumping around with pleasure. "Getaway!" snapped the Prince. "I don't want you now."

The poor little dog, who didn't understand this at all, pulled at the prince's waistcoat to make him at least look at her, and this made Prince Edward so cross that he gave her a hard kick. Instantly the bracelet pricked him sharply as if it had been a pin. He was very much surprised, and sat down in a corner of his room."The Pixie must be laughing at me," he thought. "Surely I have done no great wrong in just pushing aside a tiresome animal! What is the good of being a ruler, after all, if I am not even allowed to kick my dog?"

"I am not making fun of you," said a voice, answered the bracelet Prince Edward's thoughts. "You have committed two faults. First of all, you were out of temper because you could not have what you wanted. Then you were cruel to a poor little animal who did not in the least deserve to be beaten."I know you are far above a little dog, but if it were right that great people should ill-treat all who are beneath them, I might at this moment beat you, or kill you, for a pixie is greater than a human. The advantage of possessing a great empire is not to be able to do the evil you desire, but to do all the good you possibly can."

The Prince promised to try and do better in the future, but he did not keep his word. In the following weeks and months, his bracelet pricked him more and more often. It gave him only a slight prick for a trifling fault, but when he was naughty it made his wrist bleed.

At last, he got tired of being constantly reminded and wanted to be able to do as he liked, so he threw his bracelet under his bed. Then he thought himself the happiest of men to have gotten rid of its pricks. He gave himself up to doing every foolish thing that occurred to him, till he became quite wicked and nobody liked him any longer.

One day, when the Prince was walking about, he noticed a young girl who was so very attractive that he made up his mind at once that he must marry her. Her name was Ella, and she was as good as she was beautiful. Prince Edward believed Ella would be delighted at the prospect of becoming queen, but she said, "Sire, I may be a shepherdess and a poor girl, but even if I were a princess, I would not marry you" "What? Do you dislike me?" asked the Prince, who was very much vexed at this answer."No, my Prince," replied Ella. "Up until recently I very much admired you. But what good would riches be to me, and all the grand dresses and splendid carriages that you would give me if the bad deeds which you now do every day made me hate and despise you?"

The Prince was very angry at this speech and commanded his officers to make Ella a prisoner at once and carry her off to his palace. All-day long the remembrance of what she had said annoyed him, but as he loved her he could not make up his mind on how to punish her. Still, thinking of how she had refused his love nagged at him so much that he found himself worked up to a furious rage. He rushed off to find her, determined that if she refused to marry him one-moment longer she would be sold as a slave the very next day.

But, when he reached the room in which Ella had been locked up, he was greatly surprised to find that she was not in it, though he had had the key in his pocket all the time. His anger was terrible, and he vowed vengeance against whoever had helped her escape. After making this proclamation he dashed to his room, but he had scarcely got into it when there was a clap of thunder which made the ground shake, and the Pixie suddenly appeared before him."I promised your father," she said sternly, "to give you good advice and to punish you if you refused to follow it. You have despised my counsel. You have gone your evil way until you are only outwardly a man; you are a monster. It is time that I fulfill my promise, and begin your punishment. I condemn you to resemble the animals whose ways you have imitated. Like the lion, you frighten the innocent with your angry roars. Like the wolf, you greedily take whatever you want. Like the snake, you betray any friend to suit your purposes. Like the bull, you are bad-tempered. Therefore, in your new form, you will resemble all these animals."

The Pixie had barely finished speaking when Prince Edward found himself in a great forest, beside a clear lake, in which he could see the horrible creature he had become. He had a lion's head, a bull's horns, a wolf's feet, and a snake's body. A voice said to him: "Behold the state which your wickedness has brought you."Prince Edward recognized the voice of the Pixie.

He turned in fury to catch her and beat her up if he possibly could, but he saw no one. The Prince thought the best thing he could do would be to get as far away from the lake as he could. At least then he would not be continually reminded of his ugliness. So he ran toward the woods, but before he had gone many yards he fell into a deep pit which had been made to trap bears. Hunters hiding in a tree leaped down and secured him with several chains. Seeing that he was a rare beast, the hunters led him into the chief city of his kingdom to be displayed in a cage as a curiosity.

All the while, he furiously bit and tore at his chains, blaming the Pixie as the cause of all his misfortunes. As they approached the town he saw that great rejoicing was being held. The hunters were told that the Prince, whose only pleasure was to torment his people, had been found in his room, killed by a thunder-bolt (for that is what was supposed to have become of him). The people had offered the crown to the former tutor of the Prince, a faithful nobleman whose name was Arnold. Arnold had tutored the Prince since he had been a child and had loved the Prince as if he had been his son. This noble lord had just been crowned king, and his rise to the throne was the cause of the rejoicing. "For," they said, "Arnold is well-known as a good and just man, and we shall once more enjoy peace and prosperity."

Prince Edward roared with anger when he heard this, but it was still worse for him when he reached the great square before his palace. There he saw Arnold seated upon a magnificent throne, and all the people crowded around, cheering and wishing him a long life that he might undo all the mischief done by his predecessor. Presently Arnold made a sign with his hand that the people should be silent. He said, "I accept the crown you have offered me, but only that I may keep it for Prince Edward, who is not dead as you suppose. A certain Pixie has assured me that there is still hope that you may someday see him again, as good and virtuous as he was when he first came to the throne. Alas!" he continued, "We may hate his faults, but let us pity him and hope for his restoration. As for me, I would die gladly if that could bring back our Prince to reign justly and worthily once more."

These words went straight to Prince Edward's heart. He realized the true affection and faithfulness of his old tutor, and for the first time reproached himself for all his evil deeds. At the same instant, he felt his anger melting away, and began quietly to think over his past life. He stopped biting at his chains. The hunters took him to a great menagerie, where he was caged along with other wild beasts. Nevertheless, he was determined to show his sorrow for his past bad behavior by being gentle and obedient to the man who had to take care of him. One day, when his keeper was asleep, a tiger broke its chains and flew at the keeper to eat him up.

"I wish I could save that man's life," the Prince said to himself. He had hardly wished this when his iron cage flew open, and he rushed to the side of the keeper, who was hopelessly defending himself against the tiger. When the keeper saw the monster also rushing toward him he gave himself up for lost, but the monster threw itself upon the tiger, chased it back into its cage, secured the door, and then came and crouched at the keeper's feet.

The keeper stooped to caress the strange creature which had done him such a great service. At the same instant, the monster disappeared, and the keeper saw at his feet a playful little dog! Prince Edward, delighted by the change, frisked about the keeper, showing his joy in every way he could. The keeper, scooping the dog up in his arms, carried hi King Arnold, the former tutor of the missing prince. King Arnold's wife, the Queen, said she would like to keep this wonderful little dog. The Prince would have been very happy in his new home if he could have forgotten that he would have been the king himself. The Queen petted and took care of him, but she was so afraid that he would get fat that she consulted the court physician, who said that he was to be fed only bread, and not even much even of that. So poor Prince Edward was hungry all day long, but he was patient about it.

One day, when they gave him his little loaf for breakfast, he thought he would like to eat it out in the garden, so he took it up in his mouth and trotted away toward a brook that he knew of a long way from the palace. There Prince Edward noticed a young girl who was trying to eat a few blades of grass -- she was so hungry. He said to himself, "I am very hungry, but I shall not die of starvation before I get my dinner. If I give my breakfast to this poor creature perhaps I may save her life."So he laid his piece of bread in the girl's hand, and she eagerly ate it up. She soon seemed quite well again, and the Prince, delighted to have been able to help her, was thinking of going home to the palace when he heard a great outcry, and turning around saw Ella, who was being carried against her will into the great house. For the first time, the Prince regretted he was no longer the monster, for if he were, then he would have been able to charge toward her captors, and rescue Ella. Now he could only bark feebly at the people who were carrying her off, and try to follow them, but they chased and kicked him away. He determined not to quit the palace until he knew what had become of Ella. "I am furious with the people who are carrying Ella off, but wasn't I the one who made her a prisoner in the first place, and wasn't I the one who intended to sell her as a slave?" he said to himself.

And the Prince found himself changed at that moment into a beautiful white dove. He remembered that white was the favorite color of the Pixie, and began to hope that he might at last win back her favor. But just now his first care was for Ella. Rising into the air, he flew round and round the house until he saw an open window. He searched every room, but in vain. No trace of Ella was to be seen. The Prince, in despair, determined to search the world until he found her. He flew on and on for several days until he came to a great desert, where he saw a cavern. To his delight there sat Ella, sharing a simple breakfast with an old hermit.

Overjoyed to have found her, Prince Edward perched on her shoulder, trying to express by his chirpings and wing caresses how glad he was to see her again. Ella, surprised and delighted by the tameness of the white dove, stroked it softly and said, though she never thought it would understand her: "I accept the gift that you make me of yourself - and I will love you always." "Take care what you are saying, Ella," said the old hermit. "Are you prepared to keep that promise?" "Indeed I hope so, my sweet shepherdess," cried the Prince, who at that very moment was restored to his natural shape. "You just now said that you would love me always. Tell me that you mean what you said, or I shall have to ask the Pixie to give me back the form of the dove which pleased you so much."

"You need not be afraid that she will change her mind," said the Pixie, throwing off the hermit's robe in which she had been disguised, and appearing before them."Ella has loved you ever since she first saw you, only she would not tell you while you became so obstinate and naughty. Now that you have repented and mean to be good, you deserve to be happy, and so now she may love you as much as she likes."Ella and Prince Edward threw themselves at the Pixie's feet, and the Prince never tired of thanking her for her kindness. Ella was delighted to hear how sorry he was for all his past follies and misdeeds and promised to love him as long as she lived.

"Rise, my children," said the Pixie, "and I will transport you back to the palace. Prince Edward shall have back again the crown he forfeited for his bad behavior."While she was speaking they found themselves in Arnold's hall, and his delight was great at seeing his dear master once more. Arnold joyfully gave up the throne to the Prince and remained always the most faithful of his subjects.

Ella and Prince Edward reigned for many years. The Prince was so determined to govern worthily and to do his duty that his bracelet, which he located under his bed and put back on his wrist, never once severely pricked him again.

CPSIA information can be obtained
at www.ICGtesting.com
Printed in the USA
BVHW041650090821
614013BV00014B/270

9 781802 139976